BURIED SECRETS

Melanie Lopata

Other Books By This Author

Acknowledgements

To Bethany Rohloff and Joseph Burditt: Thank you for being beta readers for this novel. Your time and input are greatly valued. I appreciate you cheering me on through the writing of this book!

To Tina Sanders: Thank you for your encouragement from day one. You gently pushed me to continue writing, and for that I am thankful.

To Aunt Deb: Thank you for helping me with ideas throughout the writing process!

To Aunt Jeannie Parmon: Thank you for your time in editing and proofreading this before publishing! Your time, keen eye, suggestions, and hard work mean the world to me!

To all my friends and family who cheered me on during the writing and editing process … *thank you, thank you, thank you!!*

Prologue

The lake was still as the sun dipped down behind the horizon. Not a sound could be heard for miles. A slight breeze kicked leaves around, causing the grass to dance.

A woman was sitting in her wooden rocking chair in a house, slowly knitting a scarf with her wrinkled hands and arthritic fingers. She wanted to finish it before the cooler weather so her grandson could wear it. He loved green, so she chose a deep forest green for the scarf. She smiled as her fingers moved. He would love the scarf, indeed.

Her chair stopped rocking suddenly as she looked up, noticing the deafening quiet around her. The house was getting dark, and she only had a small lamp on. She stood up and stretched. How long had she been rocking? Why was the house so quiet? Where had everyone gone? Was she supposed to be doing something? She couldn't remember.

She carefully padded her way to the window and moved the curtain aside. The vast lake sat before the house, dark and still, but somehow beckoning her outside.

She grabbed her cane and walked outside, down the porch steps and across the lawn towards the dock. She still had her slippers on her feet, but she couldn't ignore the tug of fear that was pulling her towards the lake.

She reached the dock and carefully stepped up. She looked around, hearing nothing but feeling a breeze. Carefully and slowly, she walked down the dock to the end and stared at the lake. So still ... so dark. She turned around to look for the boy—where was he?—and only saw the two-story lake house which now suddenly looked uninviting. How she wished she were back in her rocking chair.

She felt herself tremble as she returned her gaze to the lake, not sure if it was from dread or trepidation. But she knew one thing: The boy wasn't outside, and he wasn't inside. Was she supposed to be watching him? He was so little.

She looked down at the water ... she stared for a minute as her mouth slowly opened. She heard a scream which lasted for minutes until she realized it was coming from her own mouth. There, on the dock looking over the beautiful lake by which she grew up—which she *knew and loved—she collapsed. Darkness fell around her, and all was quiet again.*

Chapter 1

The gravel driveway stretched on forever, it seemed, surrounded by trees and backed by mountains. The sun was still high, but clouds were slowly moving in. Thankfully, there was no rain called for in the forecast. I would have hated for my first night at the lake house to be rainy. A little rain was okay, as long as it didn't rain all summer. July was only a few weeks away, and that was usually the best month to be at the lake.

I finally reached my destination, turned the engine off, and stepped out of the car. Then I stood there, daring my feet to move.

Why couldn't I move?

The soft breeze from the trees blew around me, and I absentmindedly pushed a piece of flyaway hair out of my eyes. That's all I could do. Time seemed to have stopped at that moment.

I thought I would easily adjust once I got out of the car and saw the house with grown-up eyes, but I just stared.

Nothing could be heard but some birds and the cries of geese. It was eerie, especially returning all these years later. Everything seemed frozen in time.

The house stood before me—watching me, waiting for

my next move. I felt a vibe I hadn't felt since … well, *ever*.

I took several deep breaths before moving forward. I *had* to move forward. This was once a place of solace—a family home where love and laughter once filled the walls. Now it was a shell filled with tragedy and secrets—a shell I didn't want anything to do with but had no choice.

I grabbed my bags from the car, leaving the boxes of food and bedding for later, and walked slowly towards the door. There were two entrances: the front, where I was heading from the driveway, and the back, which looked out to the lake.

I carefully climbed the steps up to the front door and stuck the key in. I had to jiggle the key for a few seconds, but the lock finally snapped, and the door slowly opened with a loud creak. *Of course there's a creak,* I thought. *This house is ancient.*

As I stepped into the front room, the musty smell hit my nose like a cannon. I waved my hand in front of my face as if that could rid of the many years of dust that had settled there. I had wondered if someone was taking care of the house while it sat empty, but apparently not. Sunlight streamed through the window at the top of the door, showing dust particles in the air.

"Grandma would never have let it get this bad," I muttered under my breath to the stale, empty room.

A blast of cold air swept through my body so fast, I almost didn't believe it happened. I backed into the door, causing it to slam, my bags dropping from my hands. *There are no such things as ghosts. There are no such things as ghosts.* I pulled in a deep breath and let it out slowly, remembering to count like my counselor had taught me years ago.

After I gathered my senses, I looked around. The house had once been a small structure with one bedroom, a living room, a bathroom, a kitchen, and a loft. My great-grandfather built it with the help of his brother.

Years later, when my grandmother inherited the house, she had my grandfather tear down the small back porch and rebuild it to fit a couple of chairs and a porch swing. He also added to the loft, separating the one sleeping area into two small "rooms" separated by a partition. Each had a twin bed and small dresser.

The ground floor held a living room, one large bedroom, a small bathroom and kitchen. From the living room, we could see the lake through the large window Grandpa had put in. The rooms were small—it wasn't a big house—but it had once been cozy.

The back door in the living room led to a porch overlooking the lake. As a kid, I loved sitting on the porch, reading or drawing in my notebook. Once my little brother came along, I didn't have much time to myself since I was either playing with him or forced to babysit. My heart lurched at the thought of my brother, but I quickly put it in the back of my mind.

I looked around the living room, noticing that the same curtains from sixteen years ago still hung on the windows— the same gross green color I could never stand. The old stuffed sofa was still there, with the matching chair nearby. I could see the age in both. An upright chair sat near the fireplace, and the place where my grandmother's rocking chair once sat was empty. I wondered what happened to it.

I walked over to the end table by the couch and picked up the framed photograph sitting next to the lamp. It was a picture of my grandparents when they were young—in their 40's maybe—and they looked so happy. I set the frame down and glanced around for more pictures but saw none. That was odd. Grandma used to have pictures of Mom, my brother, and me all over the room. What happened to them?

I left that room and ventured to the kitchen. Flipping the switch on to light the room, and feeling thankful that the electricity worked, I noticed how out-of-date it was: faded yellow and white tile flooring, peeling wallpaper, and old appliances. I smiled at the sight of the old stove to the right of the refrigerator. Many summer meals had been cooked on that stove. Despite everything, the kitchen was cozy and still had the small table in the corner. Unfortunately, there was no microwave. My daughter would not be happy about that.

My heart gave a flutter—a nervous one at that—when I thought of my kids. They'd be here in a few days, so I had to hold it together, push my nerves back, and get the place ready. My son, young and innocent as he was, wouldn't care about a little dust or grime, but Morgan—well, let's say she was a different breed altogether. I planned on them helping me with the cleaning, but I had to at least make the place decent for them to sleep in.

I opened a few of the cupboards only to find cobwebs and dust. "I guess I need to clean soon," I muttered to the empty room. Cleaning could wait. I needed to bring in the boxes from the car and get settled before night fell.

* * * * *

The loons called out with their mournful cries, and crickets flit across the grass, chirping as they did so.

A lovely moon, brilliant and full, poised in the sky. Reflections of the moon spread across the still water, and I was mesmerized at the sight. It was like looking at a painting. Trees lined the lake, and mountains stood in the distance. The sight was breathtaking.

I was so at peace as I slowly swayed back and forth on the swing while admiring the lake. There had been two chairs on the porch, which I moved because I wanted the swing back. I had to clean it off, but it had miraculously been in good shape sitting on the side of the house.

The air was cool, and I was glad I was wearing my sweatpants and sweatshirt. I loved cool evenings like this in the summer.

My thoughts began to trail back … back … back in time …

"Are you sure you won't be missed?" James almost looked frightened, as if he had to worry about some big, bad father who would

beat him if he brought his daughter home late. I almost laughed.

"No," I cooed, touching his arm and trailing my fingers up to his firm muscles. My body gave a shiver. Could this be the night? Could tonight be the night we declare our love for each other once and for all? I waited all summer for this, and in a few short weeks I'd be back to school, and James would be back home. Tonight just has to be the night.

James leaned in and kissed me gently, his hand caressing my back. I moved in closer to him, feeling the hard ground beneath me and wishing we had more than a thin blanket to sit on.

The night was perfect: bright stars danced in the sky, surrounding the full moon, and it was so quiet but for the crickets ... and our breathing.

"Ellie ... " James gently pushed me back, taking a breath. He leaned back and stared at the sky.

I laid down next to him, rubbing his firm abs. What was he worried about? Didn't he want me? We have dated since last summer. We have known each other since I was young and began coming here with my parents. We've always been close. Was I not desirable?

"James, shh, it's ok," I whispered, kissing his earlobe. He was simply perfect. Perfect blue eyes, perfect dark hair, perfect body ...

"Ellie," he said as he turned to face me. "I want ... I want this to be special. I don't want you to do something you'll regret. You're barely sixteen."

I laid back, sighing. There it was—my age. I spoke without looking at him. "I am grown up enough to make my own decisions, James."

He laughed—actually laughed! "Sweetie, I'm eighteen. I could be thrown in jail. It's called statutory rape. What are you in a big hurry for, anyway?"

I sat up and folded my arms in anger. "So, in the meantime, you can have sex with any girl you want who is over eighteen, is that it?"

James sat up and held me close. Why was he rejecting me? "Ellie," he whispered. "I love you, and I'm willing to wait for you. I don't want there to be any regrets. Let's just be ... ok?"

I turned to him, partially pouting. I knew I was acting like a spoiled child, but I couldn't help it. I nodded anyway, and he kissed *me again, this time not as long or passionately. Oh, well. We still had the rest of the summer. Maybe he'd change his mind.*

I opened my eyes, coming back to the present. "Oh, James," I murmured. "Whatever happened to you?"

The breeze around me picked up, and I shivered. I couldn't think about the past anymore. It was hard being at the lake house, where too many memories remained, but I had to push forward. The deal was to spend the summer here with my kids and make sure the house was ready to sell in the fall, then I could put everything behind me once and for all. Besides, James was long gone. I was sure his family didn't even have their cottage next door anymore.

I finally went to bed, pushing the past out of my mind and setting my heart on the future.

Chapter 2

"Mommy! I missed you!"

I grinned and knelt as my son ran over to me, arms wide open for a hug. I nuzzled my face into his sweet little neck and savored his smell. I missed my kids. It had only been two days but longer than we've ever been apart. We are usually never apart, but I insisted I get to the lake house first in case it wasn't livable or sound. I hadn't been up here in sixteen years and didn't know what to expect.

"Let me look at you. Oh, I think you grew a little since we last saw each other!"

"Mommy!" Connor laughed. "It's only been *some* days."

"I know, honey. I've just missed your face."

"It was a long drive," Connor said, "but I didn't complain at all."

"I'm glad. I know it was a long drive. You must be hungry."

"So, this is it?"

I looked up as Morgan walked over to us with a bored expression on her fifteen-year-old face. *Ahh, I missed that face, too,* I thought sarcastically.

"Hi, sweetie. Yep, this is it." I gave her a hug, which she half-heartedly returned. She was apparently "too old for hugging." I let go of her and walked to the Jeep that had brought my kids up to me. Mason Brown was hauling their bags out of the back, and I called the kids over to help.

"Hello, Elise. Nice old place you got here," Mason said, nodding up to the house. He was one of the few people who called me "Elise" instead of "Ellie", but I didn't mind.

Mason looked up at the house, squinting with his eyebrows furrowed. "Thought it was just goin' to be you and the kids this summer. You got company?"

"What? No, it's just us," I responded slowly, wondering why he was asking.

"Oh, ok. My old eyes must be playing tricks on me. Thought I saw someone in the window upstairs," Mason chuckled.

My blood went cold. I willed myself not to turn around and look at the house. I had seen enough scary movies to know better. You know, someone looks up at a house and sees a face in the window. Creepy.

I cleared my throat and forced a smile. "Mason, thanks again for bringing them up. Are you sure you can't stay?"

"No, ma'am, but thank you. Want to get on the road before it starts to get dark. My Bessie won't want to stay home alone tonight."

I nodded in understanding. Mason and Bessie were our next-door neighbors back home—like grandparents to my kids—and Bessie didn't like staying alone. Too bad she couldn't make the drive up; she didn't like long car rides, either. The lake house was a good six-hour drive from where we lived.

"Well, give her a hug for me. We'll be back in a few months. Look after the house for me, ok?"

"Sure thing. You know we always do."

I didn't know what I'd do without him or Bessie in my life. They were family to us. They watched the kids when Morgan was younger and not able to babysit yet. They had us over often for dinner and game nights and were great friends.

After slipping Mason some money for gas, the kids and I exchanged hugs with him and waved as he drove down the driveway back to the highway.

"Mom, come *on*. I want to unpack," Morgan whined.

I turned as my daughter made her way to the house, and I couldn't help rolling my eyes a little. Impatient little mite, she was.

Connor bounded over with his backpack and overnight bag, grinning from ear to ear. "I'm ready. Let's check it out!"

I followed quickly behind, carrying the rest of their bags and briefly forgetting about the supposed "person" in the window.

"Wow, this is … gross," Morgan said when she set foot in the house.

"Don't be rude," Connor told his sister. "It was our great-grandma's house, right, Mom?"

"It was *my* great-grandma's house, actually. It's old, but it was home every summer. Lots of memories here."

Connor stuck his tongue out at his sister, who just rolled her eyes. They began to look around, and I hung back to let them explore before we went up to the loft. Connor thought everything was "super cool" and "old," while Morgan looked less than interested. I had to admit, it *was* old-fashioned—not something a teen would be excited about—but it was a family house, and we were going to spend the summer here, fix it up, and sell it, so I never, ever had to put foot in it again.

Chapter 3

It was after 8 p.m. when I was finally able to get some quiet time. The kids were in their rooms, which had been an eventful task. Morgan hated the idea of sleeping in the loft area—so close to her brother—even though she had her own room. She argued that since the space was only divided by a partition, it wasn't technically a room. I ignored her at that. She had her privacy; what more did she want? No way was she getting the large room downstairs.

I poured a glass of pinot grigio and settled onto the porch swing. It had been a long day, getting the kids settled in and unpacking more boxes that I found in my car.

I sipped my wine as I thought about Morgan's complaints regarding the internet service out here, which was spotty at best. Well, tough. I brought the kids out here because we needed this. Ok, I needed to fix the house up to sell it, but we also needed the summer to relax and reconnect. Morgan and I had never been truly close as mother and daughter, but since Greg died last year—well, she has been downright difficult. Each day, I felt like she was slipping further away from me. I wasn't sure if that was because Greg had died or if it was just a teenage thing. I didn't think I had been like that as a teenager. Then again, my mother and I weren't close, either.

A gentle breeze blew through the air, which was a welcome relief from the hot day we had, and the moon was still shining on the water. *This,* I thought, *is bliss. I could get used to it. Well, I could get used to the peace … not this place, in particular.*

I was just taking another sip of wine when I heard a scream. *Crap—what now?* I set my wine glass down and hurried inside, hearing another scream. Back home, I rarely had a peaceful evening because one of the kids either had a friend over or wanted to go somewhere. When it was just us three, there were often arguments between Morgan and Connor. I get it; there was the age difference. But sheesh. Couldn't they try to make it work? I thought I'd get at least a little peace at the lake house. Apparently, I thought wrong.

Inside, the kids were standing on the landing of the loft, looking like they had seen a ghost. But … there were no such things as ghosts, right? That's what my mother always told me.

Connor hurried down the steps and ran into my arms.

"Mom, we heard a crash," Morgan told me, her voice trembling slightly.

"It was scary," Connor mumbled into my shoulder.

"It's ok, honey." His hair smelled like shampoo from his bath that evening, and his skin was soft against mine. "What happened?"

"I told you. We heard a crash," Morgan snapped.

"Morgan, chill. Tell me where the sound came from." I was getting tired of her disrespectful attitude. Teenager or not, enough was enough.

"The basement, I think."

My veins turned to ice, and I shuddered.

"Are we going to check it out?" Morgan asked.

"Morgan, I'm not going down there this late. I'm sure it was just an animal. I'll check it out tomorrow morning." I shuddered at the thought of creeping down into the basement at night—or *any* time.

I could tell Morgan didn't like that answer, and I felt Connor trembling in my arms. I stood up, feeling my own body shake. The kids didn't know, but the basement was really just a dug-out room that was very small ... and very creepy. I had seen it once in my life, and that had been enough. I wasn't even sure what remained down there, but I wasn't about to look in the dark.

"Look, you heard a crash, but there's no noise now. It could have come from anywhere. We don't just have this house; there's a shed and outbuilding too. Let's try to sleep tonight and not worry."

Morgan groaned, and I felt like doing the same. What had I been thinking? I was out in the middle of nowhere with my kids and no protection. I didn't hate guns but didn't trust them with a five-year-old kid. I knew there were neighbors, but the closest used to live on the other side of the woods that lined our property, and I wasn't sure that the family still owned the cabin.

After calming them down with cupcakes and milk, the kids went back to their rooms to read or listen to music, and I went back to the porch.

Chapter 4

I left the curtains open when I went to bed, and in the morning, the sun was shining through. It looked like it was going to be a beautiful day. I hurried to get dressed and to the kitchen so I could make a big breakfast for the kids. I figured we'd be eating a lot of cold cereal and bagels for breakfast during the summer, so I did plan on making eggs and pancakes on occasion for a treat.

They had beat me to it. Morgan and Connor were already in the kitchen, eating toast and cold cereal. At least Morgan had made coffee. I had forgotten to set the timer and was annoyed at myself, thinking I had to wait for it to brew! Thank God for small favors. I had taught Morgan early on how to measure the coffee in the coffee maker. Sometimes I let her have some, too.

"Gee, I was going to make you two a nice big breakfast," I commented as I poured myself a generous cup of coffee.

"Sorry, Mom," Morgan mumbled, her mouth full of cereal. "We wanted to get outside early. It's warm out already!"

"Can we go to the beach today?" Connor begged. "Please?"

"Connor, don't talk with your mouth full!" Morgan chastised, glaring at her brother.

"You did!" he shouted, and cereal sprayed from his mouth.

Feeling an argument coming on, I handed Connor a napkin. Kids *were* gross sometimes.

"We can go to the beach, but I thought we'd go exploring first. There's a beautiful trail in the woods where we can hike, and—"

"Can't we go swimming?" Connor whined.

"Yes," I huffed, slightly frustrated. "I just thought we could look around first."

"Let's go swimming first. It's hot."

It *was* pretty warm already. I pulled my hair away from my face, fanning myself with my hand. I knew I should have cut my hair before summer, but I liked it long.

"Fine. Let me eat first."

"Hey, Mom," Morgan said with a mouth full of cereal, forgetting that she just lectured her brother on talking with *his* mouth full. "Are you going to check out the basement today?"

"I guess," I muttered.

All of a sudden, a cold blast shot through my body. What was with this place? Maybe there was a draft somewhere. I'd have to comb the house carefully before putting it on the market. The kids didn't notice anything as I rubbed the goosebumps on my arms. Despite the warmth of the kitchen, the cold blast did nothing to cool me off. If anything, it just freaked me out.

Ignoring the weird feeling I just had, I stuck some bread into the toaster and took a sip of my coffee. I loved the hot liquid, even on a warm day.

"So, pretty soon, the town will be holding their annual Fourth of July celebration," I told the kids, hoping to get them excited about being up here. Connor grinned; Morgan only nodded.

"Will there be fireworks?" Connor asked eagerly.

"Oh, yes. I'll have to check to see if they're doing the barbecue beforehand, but I don't see why they wouldn't. There's also a big parade and games around the park." I remembered how much fun I had when I was younger—even as a teenager! The Fourth of July get-together was a big deal in town. A barbecue with tons of food, games, fireworks ... it was amazing. And everyone came together and got along so well. That was one of the things I looked forward to most about summers at the lake house.

"Yay!" Connor dumped his cereal bowl into the sink and took off. "I'm getting my swim trunks now!"

I laughed and shook my head. Morgan remained silent as she finished her breakfast, and by the time she was done, I was sitting down with my toast. Not even ten minutes later, both kids came running downstairs.

"Ready!"

I jumped at the sound of Connor's voice. "What? I barely finished my toast!"

"Mom!" Morgan stomped into the kitchen wearing jean shorts so short they should be illegal *(when did she get those?)* and a bikini top well-filled out. *Good Lord, my baby isn't a baby anymore.* "We're ready *now!* I can watch Connor."

"No!" I hadn't meant to shout, but that's how it came out. I didn't want my kids alone in the water, especially Connor.

Morgan narrowed her eyes and then let out a huge sigh while stomping out of the room towards the back porch. Then there was the slamming of the door. Wonder where she got her temper from.

Whatever. I couldn't believe her mood lately. Ok, her mood since Greg died last year. They were never close—never really connected—but he was the "calm one" while I was the "mean mom." I usually let her moods go. I mean, what could I do? I felt like I didn't understand my own daughter most of the time.

I sat at the table, head in hands, trying to count to ten. I didn't want her mood to ruin my day. I finished my toast and grabbed another coffee, then began to fill a beach bag with towels and water bottles. Half an hour later, as promised, I was ready.

Connor eagerly followed me out the back door, and we stepped outside into the heat. The sky was vivid blue, and the sun was shining brightly on us. Connor ran ahead to the beach, where Morgan was already waiting, excited to get in the water.

Our back lawn led to rocks that edged the water. Many were large and jagged, so we didn't swim there since there wasn't a real beach area there. Our private beach was located a short distance from the house, still on land that my family owned and in full view of the house. My grandparents used to have a canoe and small boat tied to the dock at the beach, but when my grandfather died, Grandma sold them. The dock, however, remained.

The kids spread their towels out, and I lathered Connor with sunscreen. Morgan insisted she already put sunscreen on, and though I thought that wasn't the truth, I let it go. Let her get a sunburn and learn her lesson.

Connor had a blow-up tube that I insisted he attach a rope to so I could tie it to the dock. I was not about to have my son be swept away by waves. He was so young and helpless! It was a joke in our family that I was overprotective, but one of my biggest fears was losing one of my children to drowning.

As the kids ran to the water, I pulled my shorts and tee off, revealing a blue one-piece bathing suit. It was low-cut but modest. I had the figure to be able to wear a bikini but being in my early thirties—and after having two kids—I felt I should be a little mom-like in front of the kids.

I spread a blanket out and sat down to read. I had the latest John Grisham book and couldn't wait to start. It was rare that I had a chance to read, and I was determined to do more of that this summer.

"Stay close, kids!" I shouted as I grabbed my book.

The morning wore on, and the kids had a blast in the

water and building sandcastles. Or attempting to build sandcastles. I held back laughter as Connor's castle crumbled because he wanted to build it "super tall." Poor kid. I had to give him credit, though. He sure was determined. Morgan laughed good-naturedly and tried to help him rebuild, but it was futile. Finally, they both gave up and ran back into the water, splashing each other happily.

I was happy to see Morgan being nice to her brother for once. I understood the age difference was a lot, but I still thought she could have more patience with him. After all, my brother had been a lot younger than me. Then again, I wasn't sure I had much patience with my own brother.

"Ellie? Is that you?"

I jumped at the sound of a man's voice. Turning slowly and looking up, I realized it wasn't *any* man—it was James, the once-love of my life, the only man who ever made my heart feel full. Handsome, wonderful James. The man I had a past with. The man I left sixteen years ago and never heard from. He stood there in khaki shorts and a short-sleeve white shirt. He had a nice tan and was very muscular.

"I—James, um, hi!" I stood up quickly, dropping my book in the process. *Oh my gosh; what is he doing here?* I didn't say anything, just stood there stupidly while James looked over at the kids. I hadn't seen him since the summer I was sixteen—the last summer we were at the house. I ran my hand over my head to make sure my hair wasn't sticking up anywhere. Ugh, that would have been embarrassing.

"I'm here for the summer. Same house," he said. "I took it over when my parents got older."

"Your parents still have the house? I mean, you … oh, how are your parents?"

"Oh, they're good. They live in Florida." James looked back at me, and his eyes bore through mine. My heart dropped to my stomach, and I wanted to pass out. *No, no, no! No more feelings! Those stopped sixteen years ago…or so I told myself. Besides, he may have a wife.* A quick glance at his ringless finger told me he did not. A girlfriend, maybe?

"Ellie, how have you been?"

"Um, good. I'm good."

"Gosh, I haven't seen you since … I mean, well, it's been a long time. I called. I sent a letter."

I stared into the eyes of the man I had fallen in love with so, so long ago. He never called, and I never received a letter. Then again, I didn't call or write, either. Before I could answer, Connor ran up to us, wet and happy as a fish in a lake.

"Mommy! I did a back flip off the dock! Morgan helped me! Did you see?" He was jumping up and down excitedly, spraying James and me with water, and I couldn't help but grin. He had Greg's smile and enthusiasm. Then, as if just realizing someone else was there, he took a quick glance at James and said, "Hi."

James smiled. "Hello there, young man. Looks like you're having fun." Connor grinned.

"Honey, show me again. I missed it." I didn't really want Connor jumping off the dock, but as long as Morgan was close by, I figured it wouldn't hurt.

"Ok!" Connor ran back to the dock to show off, and James and I stood in awkward silence.

"Your kids … " James let his sentence trail off.

"Yeah." I knew I should have said more, but I was feeling awkward. I shouldn't have felt that way.

I had known James since I was five years old and he had been seven. We met through our families since they lived on the other side of the woods—just a trail walk away. We had practically grown up together! How many cookouts and lazy days on the beach had we shared? I couldn't count them. So many fun memories …

Ignoring the summersaults in my stomach, I watched Connor do a back flip into the water and applauded him. He grinned and kept on swimming while Morgan, thankfully, kept a careful eye on him. She was sitting at the end of the dock, her legs swinging back and forth, while watching her brother. She only glanced back at us once but didn't seem interested in the "stranger" I was talking to.

"Well, I better get going. I saw your car from the road and wanted to check in."

I turned to face James and just stared. I loved this man once. I loved him more than life itself. I never stopped loving him. And now, once again, I was going to let him walk away.

"Well, maybe I'll see you around." And with that, he walked up the hill and out of sight.

* * * * *

"Come on, Connor, you're too slow!"

"Morgan, leave him alone," I snapped.

I was irritated, hot, and had several bug bites. We were traipsing through the woods on the trail my grandfather had made for us, and I didn't remember it being so miserable. It was nearing four in the afternoon, so maybe we were just tired and hungry. Yay, me, for suggesting a hike in the woods after a long day spent at the beach.

"Mom, look!" I heard Connor shout from behind us, and as I turned, I caught him grabbing a green leaf he should not be touching.

"Connor, no!"

Too late. He had already rubbed it around in his hands, inspecting it and touching it to his face to smell it. *Poison ivy. Oh, great.* I hurried over to my son, Morgan at my heels, as Connor began to scratch at his arms. Yup—he was going to be quite a joy for the next twenty-four hours.

"Do not touch!" I scolded, scooping Connor into my arms, careful not to touch too much of his skin. I hurried as fast as I could down the path towards the cottage. *Damn it; this is the last thing I need.*

"Mom, wait up!" Morgan whined from behind.

"Morgan, we need to treat this so your brother won't itch, or it will spread."

Connor was squirming in my arms, and I gripped him

tighter. We finally made it back to the cottage, Connor now wailing in agony as the rash spread, and I set him down on the couch while I ran to the bathroom for the first aid kit. *There must be calamine lotion in this darn kit.* I was sure I had packed it!

"*Mommmm!!*"

Ugh. I was sure Connor was itching like a madman now. Where was that darn lotion? I didn't know what else to do. Ok, no lotion. I'd have to run to the store. I really didn't want to leave Morgan and Connor alone. I had left them alone on occasion after Greg died if I had to run to the store or post office quickly, but our neighbors were right next door to keep an eye on the house. Out here, with the water and woods … well, no, thank you.

"Ok, baby, I don't have any lotion, but I'm going to set these wet, cool cloths over your arms."

I stopped dead in my tracks. My son had itched his arms to the point of near-bleeding, and now he had red marks on his face too!

"Connor!"

"It itched, Mom," he moaned. I grabbed his hand before he could touch his face again. Morgan sat in the corner by the window, and I swear she had a smirk on her face.

"Morgan," I snapped. "Please go through some of the totes that haven't been unpacked yet and find that calamine lotion. I know I brought it!"

Morgan didn't look happy, but she did as she was told anyway. What a great way to start our vacation.

Chapter 5

The kids were outside—Morgan on the porch, playing a game on her cell phone that hadn't required Wi-Fi, and Connor playing with his trucks, occasionally scratching his poison ivy bumps. He had stopped itching—for the most part—and we were chilling out, so I decided it was time to look in the basement.

I walked into the kitchen and stared at the door next to the pantry. *Do I really want to do this?* I thought with a shudder. "Don't be such a baby, Ell," I muttered to myself, grabbing a flashlight.

The doorknob seemed stuck, so I had to twist and pull a few times before, finally, it loosened enough for me to open. As soon as the door swung open, I began coughing. It smelled musty and ... *old*. Taking a deep breath, I switched the flashlight on and pointed it down. There were only six steps—all wooden and rickety-looking—and they led to a black hole.

"Here goes," I said to the darkness.

With each step, my body trembled. Why was I so scared? There was no way into the basement except inside the house. And, really, it was such a small space. Surely no one could be down there.

Step by creaky step, I slowly descended into the damp hole, dark but for my small light. Finally, I made it to the bottom and shone the light around. There was a small fuse box to my left, a few old-looking boxes stacked in front of me, and sitting along the cement wall to my right was an old, beaten-up desk. I had no memory of that desk. Weird. Probably belonged to my grandparents or maybe my mother.

Well, that was it. No animals or intruders hiding in the darkness. Not that I could see, anyway. And I was certainly not going to go further and look behind boxes or feel along the wall for a secret entrance. (Did those really exist?)

I shook my head and turned to leave, and suddenly, I felt something brush across my ankle. Without thinking, I screamed and dropped the flashlight, spinning around fast to get up the steps. I lost my footing and missed the step, falling to my knees. I reached behind myself to retrieve the flashlight when I saw a shadow on the wall by the desk.

"Hello?" I called out. How stupid. Of course there was no one down there with me. But isn't that what you do in scary movies? Call out to the murderer?

I stood frozen, seeing a shadow looming over the desk. As quickly as I spotted the shadow, it disappeared. I crept forward to get a better look.

The desk was small—probably the perfect size for Connor—with a single drawer in the middle. The wood was marked up from years of use, and there were words etched in the top. I leaned closer for a better look, but I couldn't make out anything legible.

Suddenly, I heard a door slam. I whipped my body around and saw that the basement door had shut. The temperature seemed to drop significantly. I decided I had had enough.

I bolted to the steps, ran up, and grabbed the door handle. It was cold as ice. I turned the handle and burst into the kitchen. Morgan was standing there with a look on her face that wouldn't leave my memory for a long time.

"Mom ... " she said, her voice shaking. "Who was screaming?"

* * * * *

On Monday morning, I woke before the kids. I grabbed one of my favorite coffee mugs, poured coffee to the rim, and tiptoed outside to enjoy the morning. The lake was still, and the birds were singing their quiet morning song. I sat on the porch swing and put my head back. The air smelled so fresh, and the sun was already warming my body. I could tell it was going to be a beautiful day.

Since my husband passed away, I hadn't had much time to relax. Even months after his death, neighbors and friends were calling or stopping over, and all I wanted was peace. The kids and I jumped back into our daily lives to keep busy, and I found I couldn't stop after that. Even when I did have a few minutes to myself, I couldn't relax; I just had to be doing something.

At the lake house, however, I was learning to relax again. I didn't have to be on the go all the time. I could actually do something for myself.

As I looked out onto the lake, I thought about the basement. I hadn't been down there since the day Morgan heard me scream when I first explored it. She insisted the scream didn't sound anything like me, but I brushed it off. Of course it was me; I know I screamed. As for looking over the basement carefully, I would have to do that another time when I either had the nerve or someone was with me. This house was old, but surely not haunted.

I had told the kids we'd go into town to get a few groceries, and I would show them around. The town wasn't anything major—just a cute tourist town with fun little shops and eateries—but it was homey, and I wanted them to see another part of my life ... or what had been my life.

The town, surrounded by two lakes, had a few motels, several eating establishments, vendors in the park, a library, a few churches—typical stuff like that. There were also fun activities for the kids throughout the summer. Nothing huge or spectacular but perfect for the area.

I was swinging with my eyes closed, enjoying the morning, when I heard something—a crash, but not inside the house. I quickly set my mug down and stepped off the porch, looking around. Not seeing anything out of the ordinary, I crept along the side of the house towards the outbuilding, which was a one-story barn-like structure where my grandparents had stored things like boxes full of items they wanted to keep, toys for us to play with during the summer, extra tables and chairs for cookouts—that sort of thing. I noticed the building the day I arrived but hadn't given it much thought.

Looking at the door, I noticed there was no lock on it, so I yanked on the handle, and the door swung open.

"Mom?"

I jumped at the sound of Morgan's voice. Turning around, I saw her and Connor, standing in their pajamas, bleary-eyed and watching me.

"What are you doing out here in your pajamas, Mommy?" Connor rubbed his eyes and yawned.

"I, um … what are *you two* doing out here?"

"We heard a noise," Morgan said. "Not that you'll believe me."

Don't roll your eyes, don't roll your eyes. Taking a deep breath, I responded, "I heard a noise, too. That's why I'm here."

"Inside?" Connor asked, pointing to the building.

I nodded. "Inside."

We crept into the enormous structure, keeping close to one another, and I noticed the wood showed signs of age. We were surrounded by darkness apart from some light seeping in from windows that sat high up towards the ceiling. *There must be a light in here.*

Morgan nudged me and pointed to a switch to my left. *Ahh, good. A light.* I flipped the switch, and when light flooded the area, we stood there staring. Junk. Nothing but piles and piles of … *stuff*. Just boxes and furniture. You could barely move in there. Why hadn't this been cleaned out after we left?

"Holy crap," Morgan murmured. I didn't chastise her for her language. I was just as surprised as she was.

We looked around, careful not to trip over anything. Old furniture and outdoor chairs—hardly useable, it seemed—some old toys, including a rocking horse, and boxes that hadn't been properly sealed. Some boxes had their contents nearly spilling out with papers like letters or bills. Others seemed warped with weather and age. Good grief. I'd have to go through all of that stuff before selling the property.

"What in the world?"

I looked to where Morgan was standing. In the far right-hand corner of the room sat my grandmother's rocking chair. I couldn't believe it was there. My grandmother always rocked in that chair inside the house, and sometimes out on the porch, but after the accident, we never saw it again. I wondered who put it in there. I couldn't believe any of the stuff still sat in this building. It haunted me. I wanted to get out.

"Whose stuff was this? Yours?" Morgan asked, looking around. She was standing by the rocking chair and reached down to touch it. That stuff hadn't been mine—not all of it. I wasn't about to get into that.

I walked over to the chair, which was very dusty, and reached to touch the handle. "This was my grandma's chair," I whispered, running my hand over the weathered piece of furniture. I hadn't seen it in years.

Suddenly, the light flickered, and a blast of cold air shot through the building. I yanked my hand away from the chair as Connor ran to the door. Morgan and I looked at each other with wide eyes. My heart was beating so fast I thought it would burst out of my chest.

"What was—"

I shook my head. "We're done here," I said before

Morgan could finish.

We hurried to meet Connor at the door, and as I reached for the light switch, I turned around to take another glance at the chair.

It was rocking.

Chapter 6

After a lunch of hot dogs and cold baked beans, I ordered the kids to get ready for our trip to town. While I cleaned up, I thought about the conversation we had over lunch.

"Mom, can we use that rocking chair?"

"Hmm?" I polished off the rest of my hot dog and wiped my mouth, looking at Morgan.

"The rocking chair. The one in the outbuilding that belonged to your grandma. Can we bring it up and set it on the porch?"

"No!"

Morgan looked taken aback for a second, then narrowed her eyes at me. "Why not?"

"Because Mommy said so," Connor piped in, his mouth full of beans.

Morgan glared at her brother. I decided on another approach.

"I was thinking maybe we can have a yard sale. You know, get rid of a bunch of stuff that we don't need."

"Cool!" Connor shouted, beans spraying from his mouth.

"Gross, Connor!" Morgan shouted. She wiped food off her arm—it was pretty gross—and tried again. "Mom, that chair would be great on the porch! Great Gran used to rock on it all the time—you said so yourself. Why can't we use it?"

I sighed. I had no argument. What was I going to tell her? "No,

I don't want it anywhere near me—too many painful memories?" I'd have to explain everything, and I didn't want to do that.

"Fine," I sighed. "But let's work on that yard sale while we're at it."

I had given in, but I wasn't happy about it. That rocking chair gave me bad, heart-breaking memories—memories I didn't want to surface. But what could I do?

I finished wiping the counter, pulled my hair into a ponytail, and grabbed my purse. Time to get to town.

* * * * *

"Why, Miss Ellie!" Gert exclaimed as she hobbled towards me. She enveloped me in a big hug, which I happily returned. I had missed her. Gert was the town gossip, but she was one of the nicest women I knew. She never gossiped to be mean or spread rumors; she just liked to know what was going on. Gert was always especially kind to our family, being close friends with my grandmother, and loved to sneak candy to my brother and me when we stopped in her store. When I was last in town sixteen years ago, Gert moved around more easily. Time sure does change people.

"I haven't seen you in, what … ten, twelve years?"

"More than that," I chuckled, pulling back and taking a look at the woman who had been like another grandmother to me. She still wore her hair up in a tight, no-nonsense bun and wore a store apron over her flowered dress. She had always lived simply, and I admired her for it.

"Oh, now, what's kept you?" Before I had a chance to reply, she went on. "Now, honey, I'm awfully sorry about your grandmother. She sure was a dear. Shame she died in the house all alone. I didn't even realize she had come back until James told me he had been—"

"Wait," I interrupted Gert's rambling. "Grandma died in the *lake house?* No one told me."

"Oh, I'm sorry, dear," Gert shook her head and took my hand. "We thought she had left … some nursing home,

I think it was. No one knew she stayed or came back." Gert took a deep breath before continuing. "James returned a few weeks later to get the place ready for the winter, and he ... well, he found her." She whispered the last part dramatically.

"What? James ... found her ... *where?*"

"Oh my! Are these your children, Ellie?" Gert exclaimed as she spotted my kids.

"Yes, this is—wait, where was my grandma found?"

"Now, what's your name, sweetie?" Gert was fawning over Connor.

The kids introduced themselves, and I had to stay quiet and patient. I wanted to know where my grandma had died, but I didn't want to push Gert further. Not when the kids were listening.

When Gert was done with her grandmotherly duties, the kids took off to look around, and I pulled on Gert's arm. "Please, Gert. Where did he find Grandma?"

"In her rocking chair in front of the living room window."

In her ... *what???* How was Grandma found dead in the rocking chair? I waited impatiently for Gert to continue, forcing myself not to tap my foot on the ground.

"Such a shame." She shook her head. "No one did an autopsy because your mother was ... is ... um, well, you know, and there was no other family around. So that was that!"

A customer walked in, interrupting our talk, so I had no choice but to wait. My heart felt heavy at what I had just discovered. My grandma ... she died alone in the house that carried death and secrets. Poor Grandma. What had she been thinking about that day while rocking in front of the window? My heart broke for her for the second time in my life.

I glanced around the small store while I waited for Gert to return to me. It hadn't changed at all since I had last been there. The wooden floors were scuffed with age. The walls and aisles were lined with shelves filled with fishing poles, groceries, personal care items, books, and anything else a tourist—or local—would need at the lake or camping. In the corner sat a gumball machine and ice cream freezer. It was a cozy store, and Gert knew nearly everyone who walked through her door.

When Gert was done with her customer, she walked back over to us, seeming to take special notice of Morgan. "How old are you, dear?"

"Fifteen—almost sixteen!" Morgan told her proudly.

"Fifteen?" Gerty's eyes narrowed as she appraised my daughter. "Well, that's just the perfect age for helping out here at the store one or two days a week, don't you think?"

"You mean *work?* Like a paid job?" she squeaked. She turned to me and grinned. Morgan loved earning money. She had many babysitting jobs back home, and I know she was disappointed to leave for the summer and lose out on a lot of money. "Can I, Mom?"

"I don't know … " I mumbled. It was different at home when she was close by and just babysitting. Was I being overprotective?

"Oh, hush." Gerty swatted my arm playfully. "I drive past your cottage every day to get here. It's no problem to pick her up and bring her back at the end of the day. My part-time boy, Michael, is here the other four days, and I could use a hand the two days he's not here and when he needs a day off here and there."

"Mom, *please?*" Morgan begged.

"Well, I guess it couldn't hurt … " I was still unsure, but Morgan looked so happy, and it would be a good experience for her.

"Awesome," Morgan said coolly, though I could tell she wanted to shriek with joy.

"Good, then it's settled." Gerty motioned for Morgan to follow her so she could show her around and talk about what she'd be doing, so I stood there waiting.

The door chimed, signaling another customer, and I

automatically looked up. James walked inside.

Oh gosh, I thought as my heart began to race. *Why do I still get jitters when he is around?* He looked amazing in fitted jeans, work boots, and a short-sleeve white shirt. His face was flushed with heat and sun, which made his blue eyes shine brighter. I was practically swooning.

James spotted me and smiled. "Ellie … hey." He walked over to me, and I smiled, trying to act casual.

"Hi, James."

"Mom, look! This car is, like, old-school!" Connor ran over to me, holding onto a vintage-looking toy car. He looked up at James and grinned. "Hello."

"Hi, there. Now who might you be?"

"I'm Connor and I'm almost six." He raised his head, trying to be taller.

"That's a great age to be. You like vintage cars?"

"What's vintage?" Connor's eyebrows furrowed.

"Old," James laughed.

"Oh, yeah! It's cool." Connor looked up at me, his eyes pleading. "Mommy, can I get it?"

"I don't see why not."

"*Yes!*" Connor bolted off in search of more "cool" cars, leaving James and I alone.

"Cute kid," James said with a chuckle.

"Thanks. Um, so what brings you to town?" *Ugh, stupid question.*

"Probably same as you." He smiled.

"Oh. Yeah." I knew I was blushing. What a dolt.

James and I stood there for a second, and I wasn't sure what to say. Of course, I finally blurted out, "So, did you bring your girlfriend with you this summer, or … ?"

James only grinned. "No girlfriend. No wife."

Phew!

"Had a few girlfriends here and there but no one special, you know?"

I only nodded. I was going to say something else, when Morgan ran up to me. "Mom, Gert said I could start tomorrow! Is that ok?"

James and I turned to look at Morgan, who had a smile on her beautiful face. James stared at her for a moment before turning to me.

"This is Morgan. Morgan, this is James. He has a cottage on the other side of the woods from ours."

"Hi," Morgan said.

They stood there for what felt like hours, sizing each other up. James with his dark hair and blue eyes; Morgan with dark hair and blue eyes. Similar features, exact same nose. The resemblance to each other was uncanny, and I know they both noticed.

"Um, so can I start tomorrow, Mom?" Morgan asked again, looking at me with a puzzled look.

"Sure, honey. Let's get what we need now, though, and get back so you two can have the afternoon to play."

"Hey," Morgan said before turning away. She looked right at James. "Maybe you can stop over later and help carry a rocking chair to the porch. It's in some old building. It's so cool and, like, ancient!"

"Grandma's chair," I explained, and James nodded, though his eyebrows were raised in surprise.

"Sure, Morgan. I can stop by later, if that's ok with your mom."

"Sure," I muttered. "Thanks."

James nodded again, and with one last look at my daughter, he walked away.

That wasn't awkward at all.

Chapter 7

The afternoon went by quickly, but the kids had fun. They played in the yard—catch and tag as well as finding "cool" rocks for Connor's collection—went swimming for a while and helped me around the house (though not without a little grumbling from the teenager). The house needed a good scrubbing and some paint here and there, but for the time being, we did general cleaning to make it cozy for our stay. I was happy that the kitchen had been kept in good shape. Kitchen grime usually grossed me out, so I always tried to maintain a spotless room. Other than dust bunnies and a lot of cobwebs ("Cool!" from Connor), cleaning was a breeze.

Morgan set some of her scented candles around the living room, and I warned her to blow them out whenever she left the room for a long period of time.

"Fires are dangerous," I explained. She just nodded, and I hoped she'd remember.

Throughout the day, I couldn't stop thinking about what Gert had told me. That hadn't really made sense. When Mom and I left the house after the accident, we knew Grandma had stayed behind to pack things up. My aunt later told me that she secured a nice room for

Grandma at a nursing home. Did Grandma sneak out of the home? Did they *let* her leave? Why had she returned to the house? None of those things seemed likely. Nursing homes were very strict … that is, if you had a good one.

Unless … Had my aunt lied to me? But why would she do that? Had she purposely kept my grandmother from me all those years? My aunt and I hadn't been close. In fact, she and my mother almost seemed estranged. Maybe my aunt thought she'd be in my grandma's will and wanted to keep us away? I also wondered why my aunt's name wasn't listed on any of Grandma's important documents. Gert made the comment about there being no other family. The questions would not stop niggling at my mind.

And did I really want that chair—the chair she *died* in—to be on the porch?? *Ugh.*

After supper that evening, we were hanging out on the porch, enjoying the sounds of the lake and the birds still singing in the trees. Morgan was trying hard to get service on her cell phone, and Connor was reading a chapter book that had belonged to me when I was his age. I loved that he loved reading and wished Morgan would read more. Then again, how much did I read at her age? I was more interested in boys and hanging out with my friends than reading.

I was just thinking I should grab my book from inside, when I heard tires on the gravel in our driveway. Connor ran to see who it was, and I continued to swing, not really caring who was visiting. I felt relaxed. That was short-lived.

"Mom! Look who's here!"

I turned when my son shouted from the side of the house, and my heart dropped to my stomach. *James.*

"Hey, Ellie. I promised I'd help with the chair, remember?" he greeted with a shrug.

No, I did *not* remember. I heaved a sigh but forced a smile. No reason to be rude.

Morgan jumped up excitedly from her spot on the steps. "Awesome!" she practically shouted.

What in the world was her obsession with that damn chair? I stood up and smiled at James. No sense in making him feel bad for something he agreed to help with.

"Hi," I greeted.

His warm smile melted me inside. *Oh, no, not all these years later!*

"Come on," Morgan said, pulling at James's arm. "I'll show you where it is. It's, like, SO cool! I thought it'd be perfect out here, overlooking the lake … " Morgan went on and on while dragging James towards the outbuilding. I heaved a big sigh. I didn't want to be near that chair. It haunted me. Grandma had been sitting in that chair the day … well, *that* day, sixteen years ago. And then she *died* in it!

* * * * *

A loon and an owl could be heard in the distance, and cicadas sang their silly songs. I've always loved the sound of loons, even when I was younger. They sounded so … mournful, yet it was comforting to me. The moon rose higher in the sky, casting an almost ghostly glow on the lake. I swung back and forth in my seat, while James sipped his drink, shooting occasional glances at me that I pretended not to notice. *Good Lord, I feel like a teenager again!*

James had brought the chair up on the porch for Morgan, and I ordered her to clean it since it was *her* idea to bring that wretched thing out of storage. She grudgingly did, and Connor helped her. While they were busy doing that, James and I moved things around in the outbuilding to try organizing things to either sell or trash.

Now it was past nine. The kids were in their rooms, and James and I were having a glass of wine on the porch. I was finally able to relax around him without my heart feeling like it would burst out of my chest. It almost felt like old times again—just relaxing and talking easily.

I learned that James lived a few hours from his own lake house (the opposite direction of my house) and was a full-time book editor. I talked about the kids but didn't talk about myself too much. He was easy to talk to and a great listener, just as he had been in the past.

As the night wore on, I felt I could ask James something that had been on my mind since returning to the lake house.

"James, do you believe in … spirits?" I took a drink from my glass, too embarrassed at the question to look at him.

"Spirits? Like ghosts?"

"No, no, like … I don't know. When people die, do you think people can return in a way to send a message?" He raised his eyebrows. "James, I am serious."

"*Okayyyyy*," he said slowly. "Sure—I think that they're allowed to reach us from beyond. I think when that happens, they're not completely at rest in the afterworld. They need to get a message through to someone or finish things here before they can rest. Make sense?"

"Mm," I mumbled, taking another sip of my wine. We sat in silence for a while. My mind was on spirits. Clearly, his wasn't.

"Ellie?"

"Hmm?"

"Do you ever … Do you ever think of that day?"

I didn't answer. Of course I thought of *that day*. Why wouldn't I? That day has haunted me for the last sixteen years and always will. It was the best day and the worst day. I'd never forget it.

James sighed at my silence. I thought he might leave or go get another drink. I could sense him staring at me, but I was reluctant to return the gaze. My hand gripped the stem of my wine glass, and it was all I could do from shaking and spilling my wine. Why did he have to bring up the past? Why couldn't we just have a nice relaxing evening and—

"Ellie, look at me."

Damn it. "James, I—"

"You're back after all these years, so it's a good time to talk."

"There's nothing to talk about!" I snapped, finally looking at him. *God, he was gorgeous.* My mind was suddenly flooded with memories: soft sand against my body, the sun beating down ... then sudden screaming in the distance—a horrible ending to a wonderful day.

"We haven't talked since the accident! I haven't seen you or spoken to you since then. Do you expect things to just go back to normal now?"

"James, please, let it all go," I whispered, shaking myself out of the memories.

James heaved a sigh. He had always been very patient, but now, he looked frustrated. "Ellie, I'm so, *so* sorry for what happened to your brother, but why didn't you return my calls ... my letter? Why did you take it out on *me?* After what we had been through that summer ... "

"I didn't get any calls or a letter!" I stood up and paced the porch, wishing I had brough the bottle of wine outside. "James, my brother *died* that day! He died because ... because I neglected him! And *you're* the one who disappeared. I wanted to call, but—"

James stood and grabbed my arm. "Ellie, that didn't happen because of what we were doing."

I looked away, staring at the lake—so still, so dark. The moon's reflection was captivating, and I was drawn to it. I set my glass down and walked across the lawn and down the slope to the rocks at the edge of the lake. Everything around me was so still, so peaceful.

"Help! Help, please! Oh God, someone help, please!"

I could still hear the screams from that day. That horrible day. The day when everything was perfect but so awful.

"Ell ... "

I turned to James as he approached, his voice near a whisper. I felt tears running down my face. The pain, the memories—it all came flooding back. James pulled me into his arms, and I melted in the embrace of the man I once loved—*still* loved. The man who was a blessing and a mistake. He held me as I cried until I had nothing left inside.

Chapter 8

The kids and I had been at the lake house for almost a week and had settled in nicely. We had made the house cozy and perfect for us and settled into a nice routine. Breakfast was sometimes pancakes and eggs and sometimes cereal, followed by cleanup and readying for the day. Morgan worked at Gert's, while Connor and I continued to clear old things out of the house but also took walks or hung out on the beach. He was always eager to hear stories from my childhood about this place and seemed to love it as much as I once had.

I hadn't seen James in a couple days, and part of me was relieved. I couldn't believe I had fallen into his arms like that—just like I used to. I refused to get involved again. It couldn't happen. I had too much to lose.

The afternoon was beautiful and warm. So far so good with the weather! I was happy about that—not just for myself but for the kids. I hadn't wanted them cooped up inside all summer.

Morgan was working at Gert's, and Connor and I had a nice walk in the woods, which, thankfully, was uneventful. I think he learned his lesson from getting poison ivy on the last hike.

"Mom?"

My son's voice jolted me out of my thoughts. I turned to see him standing expectantly in the doorway of the kitchen, where I had just cleaned up from lunch. He was wearing his swim trunks and holding onto his goggles.

"I guess you want to take a break and go swimming," I chuckled, taking him into my arms. He was so small, so innocent. I wished that innocence would last forever.

"Mom, you're smooshing me," he said, wriggling out of my arms with a giggle.

"Sorry. Ok, let me grab my stuff, then we'll head out." I finished wiping the counter and from the corner of my eye saw Connor walking down the hall. "Connor! Don't go outside without me!" I shouted frantically.

I tossed the rag into the sink and hurried into the hallway. Connor was standing by the front door, a confused look on his face. He reminded me of my younger brother, Johnny, when he was alive—his face so innocent and carefree.

"Honey, wait for me, ok?"

Connor nodded, and I ran to my room to change. After pulling my suit on, I grabbed some towels, sunscreen, and a magazine I was sure I wouldn't read, then hurried to the kitchen to grab water bottles.

When I came out of the kitchen and headed to the back door, my son was not there. My heart began beating wildly in my chest. I called his name and looked through the house, but there was no Connor. I shouted his name. No answer.

I thought my heart was going to explode. I told him to stay put! Not seeing him anywhere, and tears filling my eyes, I threw the back door open, while yelling his name, and ran right into James.

"Ellie! Slow down!"

"James! I can't find Connor!" I shouted, frantically shoving him aside.

And there he was—my son, looking sheepish, sitting on

the swing.

"*Damnit*, Connor! You *cannot* do that! I told you to stay put!" I shouted.

Connor began to cry, and James tugged at my arms. "Hey, Ellie," he said, trying to get me to look at him.

"He could have drowned!" I screamed. I was shaking all over, and I could feel sweat prickling at my skin. My heart thudded so hard, I thought I might have a heart attack.

At that point, my son was bawling, and I was in tears myself. I had to get a grip. I pulled out of James's grip and went to my son, pulling him into my arms. His hair, his skin—it smelled so sweet. My sweet boy.

"I'm sorry, Mommy," Connor said, sniffling and trying to wipe tears away.

"Honey, you can't leave the house without someone watching you. You're so young!" I tried to keep my voice calm. I was shaking all over. Maybe I had overreacted a little, but given the past I had gone through, I didn't want a repeat.

"Mommy! I'm a big boy."

I pulled away and looked at my son. "Yes, yes, you are. But I still need to look after you, ok? Water can be dangerous for anyone if they're alone. Even adults. Do you understand?" I felt a little bad then. I never wanted my son to feel he was anything but strong and brave, yet at the same time, he needed to understand he was young and still needed someone to look after him.

Connor nodded and wiped his nose with his arm.

I stood up shakily and looked at James. His face was— well, I couldn't tell what he was thinking. I had acted like a lunatic. I knew that.

"Let's head to the beach, shall we?" I said with false cheer after taking a deep breath.

Connor stood, and the three of us headed to the beach, Connor running ahead, quickly getting over the fact that his mother just wigged out. James and I lagged back, watching him. I still wasn't sure why James was at my house. I was surprised he came back since I had broken down and cried in his arms.

"Ell … " James said softly. I didn't dare look at him. "You can't do that. It's not fair to Connor."

Even though James spoke in a soft voice, I was seething inside. I turned to him and mustered the dirtiest look I could imagine. "Are you kidding me? It takes *seconds* for a child his age to drown," I spat. "I will not lose him! *You*, of all people, should get that." And with that, I stormed away from him and settled closer to the water's edge. I would never take my eyes off my son again.

I'm not sure when James left, but Connor splashed around for nearly an hour, while I sat with my knees to my chest, watching him. The sun beat down on me and I realized I had forgotten to put sunblock on both of us, but I didn't care. As long as Connor was safe, I was happy.

I still couldn't believe I had acted like that with Connor disappearing on me. I was so afraid of my kids being in or near the water without me watching them. Wouldn't any mother act that way after losing a loved one to drowning?

After a while, I called Connor to get out of the water. He obeyed but didn't look happy about it.

"Aw, Mom," he whined. "Why do I have to?"

"It's been over an hour! Let's go get a snack. I need to make some coffee," I told him. *And Mommy is baking in this sun,* I thought.

Connor reluctantly walked over to me. I handed him a towel, and he began to dry off. "Mommy? Why are you afraid of the water?"

I looked at my son curiously. "Why would you think that?"

Connor shrugged. "You seem scared of it. You don't want me and Morgan to go in alone, and you're always worried about drowning."

I sighed and put my arm around Connor's shoulders. "I'm not scared of water. I like swimming. I'm just paranoid, that's all. I'm sorry about earlier."

Connor nodded, and we walked back to the house. I hadn't told Connor about my brother's accident that happened many years ago. I didn't want him to be afraid of the water or ask questions, so I never said a word.

Morgan would be home soon, and I wanted to relax before she did. I made Connor a fun snack of "ants on a log," which was raisins on top of peanut butter that was spread over celery sticks. He loved that snack, and I was hoping he'd forget the earlier incident of me yelling.

While he ate his snack, I made some coffee and headed outside. The day was still warm and sunny. I sat on the swing and gently pushed myself back and forth using my feet. I wondered what James thought of me now. I didn't care, really. I'd do anything to protect my son, and if that meant scaring him into never leaving the house alone, then so be it.

I had been this way since my brother drowned. Greg understood; he got it. Whenever we took the kids to the beach, he let me act overprotective and went along with it. Bless his heart—Greg never complained or questioned my actions.

Suddenly, I heard my cell phone ring inside the house and was a little surprised, as service was spotty in the woods. After six rings, it stopped. I heard Connor's footsteps as he came out onto the porch, still wearing his swim trunks.

"Honey, why don't you change?" I suggested as he sat next to me.

"Don't want to. Here." He handed me my phone.

"Oh, thanks." I took the phone and looked at the screen. *Ugh,* I thought. I didn't want to listen to the voicemail. I knew who had called, and this was my vacation; I didn't want to deal with it.

"Who was it?" Connor asked.

"No one important." I set my phone down beside me and put my arm around my son. We swung for a while and soon heard a car pulling into the driveway. Morgan ran to the porch to greet us, wearing jeans, a blue short-sleeve top, and sneakers, her hair in a ponytail. She also had a big grin on her face.

"Mom, you will not believe what happened today!"

"Good day at work, huh?"

"The best! So, these guys came in—well, boys, like my age—anyway, they were buying stuff, and one boy started talking to me. He's, like, *so* cute!! His name is—"

"Whoa!" I interrupted, holding my hand up. I stood up from the swing and faced my daughter. "A boy? You met a boy?"

"Um, yeah, that's what I'm telling you," she huffed.

"Morgan, you're only—"

"Yes, Mother. I'm fifteen. And a lot of girls my age have been dating for years!"

"Well, you're not 'other girls' and I'm not going to let you hang out with boys you don't know."

"His name is Brian, and he is *so* nice. Gert knows his parents. Come on, Mom! He and his friends and some other girls are going to the public beach this weekend and invited me."

"Morgan, I don't know any of these kids, nor do I know their parents. This is not up for debate."

"But—"

"No!"

Morgan glared at me before stomping into the house, slamming the door behind her. I heaved a sigh and sat down. Connor rubbed my back with his little hand. This was not the way I had planned our summer to go. And, to make things worse, my phone began to ring again. I knew I couldn't avoid this phone call forever. When Connor walked inside to get his toys, I finally called back just to get it over with.

"We've been trying to reach you. I thought you forgot about the monthly check-in," the voice on the other end of the line said in a clipped tone.

"Sorry," I mumbled, not really sorry but saying it

anyway. I took a sip of my now-cold coffee and set my head back on my chair. The sun still cast its rays onto the water which was absolutely beautiful. The ambiance would have been completely peaceful if not for the phone call I had to endure.

"Anyway, June had a rough spot early on in the month, but she's been fine." The head nurse who called me was Rolanda, and, though she was nice, I dreaded these conversations. I never wanted them, but those were my aunt's terms when my mother was committed all those years ago.

"What happened?" I asked but didn't care much. My mother had been in a near catatonic state since I was sixteen. It was almost as if she were dead. Don't get me wrong—I love my mother, but we have never been close, and after the accident all those years ago ... well, my mother was lost to me.

"One of the nurses heard her mumble a name, and the nurse realized she was speaking of you," Rolanda explained.

I sighed. "What did the nurse tell her?"

"Why, she simply said she was sure you were having a wonderful summer at the lake house."

I sat up so fast that coffee sloshed out onto my lap. "Damn!"

"What is wrong?" Rolanda asked sharply. "That *is* where you are, isn't it?"

"Yes, but that was only for staff to know in case of an emergency. That could set my mother back, or even—"

"Relax, she's fine now. She didn't initially take the news well—supposedly yelling things the nurses couldn't understand—but after some sedation, she was fine. She asked for a pencil and some paper, and—while being observed, of course—she drew some pictures and wrote some notes. I think that's progress."

I rolled my eyes, happy that Rolanda couldn't see me. Mother drawing or writing was not progress. But at least she calmed down after hearing I was at the lake house.

Hearing that could have been very damaging to her. The last words my mother ever spoke to my grandmother were that we would never, ever be coming back to the lake house and that it should be burned to the ground. After my brother's funeral, she stopped talking.

Rolanda continued to update me on things, and when we ended our call, I walked back into the quiet house. It was after eight, and Connor was sound asleep, tired from swimming and running around all day. Morgan was in her room, probably on her iPad or phone, trying to get service. I'm sure she wasn't actually reading a book.

After refilling my mug, I walked back out to the porch and down the steps towards the edge of the lawn near the rocks. It really was a beautiful and peaceful place. During the summers I had been at the lake house, my family and I would sit on the porch or on a blanket on the lawn and talk and tell stories while gazing out at the lake. In my younger days, I would run around, trying to catch fireflies. I never did catch one, but it was fun to try. My mother was usually distant, off in her own world, but I loved hearing stories told by my grandparents. Even Johnny had some fun things to talk about once he learned to talk. His favorite thing to do was search for bugs in the grass and try to name them.

I sat down on the grass and looked up at the sky. Closing my eyes, I let the past pull me back …

"See you later, Grandma! Johnny is on the porch, playing with his trucks. I'll be back later!" I ran out the door before my grandmother could reply. I tossed my beach bag over my shoulder, threw on my beach hat, and hurried across the lawn. I wasn't about to get caught watching my little brother like I always did. I turned around to look at the house before continuing. Johnny sat on the floor of the porch, zooming his little trucks around. He was a good little boy; I just was tired of Mom always pawning him off on me. Why was she always going into town, anyway?

I continued across the lawn until I reached the edge right before the woods. I hurried down a small slope to an almost-hidden beach area that James and I had found last summer. That was our spot—a spot where we could be alone with no adults bothering us and no little brother annoying us. We couldn't be seen from there, as the beach was nestled into the hill. You could even put your feet in the water without being seen.

James was waiting for me. He had a blanket spread out and a small radio sitting nearby that was playing country music. I set the bag down and threw myself into his arms. He kissed me long and hard, his hand trailing down my back.

"James," I giggled, pushing him away. "There will be plenty of time for that. Now, look what I brought." I reached into my bag and pulled out a bottle of cheap brandy I found in one of Grandma's cupboards.

James grinned and grabbed the bottle. "Just a little, now. We need to be responsible."

I grinned back. This was going to be an amazing day.

Chapter 9

The day passed without too much conflict between Morgan and me, but I could feel some tension. She was still upset with me for not letting her go to the beach with new friends, and I felt bad, so I finally called Gert to get her opinion.

"Oh, honey," Gert said after I explained the situation. "I know those kids well—their parents, too. They're a good bunch. You need to let her have fun this summer and make new friends. Your mother would have allowed you to, you know."

"My mom never cared what I did," I mumbled.

"What's that, dear?"

"Nothing. It's just different up here. At home, I know her friends and the boys she hangs out with. But if you think she'll be safe, then I guess it will be fine. I mean, there are lifeguards at the beach, right?"

"Of course, dear. She'll be fine."

I thanked Gert and hung up, feeling a little better. I was about to go to Morgan's room and tell her the good news, when I heard the mail truck coming up the driveway, so I waited so I could grab the mail.

"Thanks, Ronnie," I called, waving to our ancient

mailman after he handed me a small stack. At least, he *seemed* ancient. Heck, he had been the mailman when I was a kid!

I sifted through the mail, seeing only bills, but at the very bottom was a letter addressed to me, and the return address caused my stomach to drop a little. My hands were shaking, but I forced myself to go into the house and leave it on the counter for now. That letter would be best opened with a glass of wine later.

* * * * *

Morgan was thrilled—no, *ecstatic*—that I was letting her go to the beach on Saturday with her new friends. She jabbered on about which suit to wear while I instructed her on what to bring: sunscreen, a towel, water, stuff like that. I hoped I wouldn't regret my decision to let her go. But Morgan wasn't a child anymore, and I couldn't keep her under my "wings" forever.

I think part of me was afraid because I remembered what I had done at her age. Morgan and I weren't terribly close, so I didn't know what boys at her school—if any— she liked, if she was thinking about sex, or stuff like that. It saddens me because I think it's my fault we aren't close. I always told myself I would never be like my mother, but I was no better than her, judging by my relationship with my own daughter.

While Morgan sifted through her things, deciding what to bring, Connor and I worked on making a list of things that needed fixing up in the house to make it sellable. I wasn't sure if anyone would really want old furniture or little figurines, but maybe I'd be surprised. After all, they do say that one man's junk is another's treasure. Maybe some were antiques, but I didn't care. I thought of myself as a minimalist and didn't want to keep what I didn't need.

I decided to call James and ask if he'd help fix or replace a few of the partially rotted porch steps. He agreed, and I was happy he didn't sound like he held a grudge from the last time we spoke. I hated how that last conversation ended—me yelling at him because I thought Connor was at the beach alone—but thankfully, James knew I was always quick to overreact. I would have to work on that, though.

James agreed to fix the steps on Saturday, so that was another thing I could check off my list.

It had taken me years to get back up to the lake house, and I wasn't about to return once we left at the end of summer. It had to be fixed up and sold before we headed back home.

* * * * *

Saturday arrived, and Morgan set off to the beach with her new friends. James had gotten to the house early, and we had coffee together before he worked on the steps. He had forgiven me for yelling, and I apologized and promised to try to "chill" a little.

I made pancakes and bacon for breakfast, which made Connor really happy, but once he found out Morgan was hanging out with friends at the public beach, he became sullen and started to complain.

"Hey, Ellie, I can take Connor fishing if he wants. Maybe that would help take his mind off his sister going to town with friends," James suggested after we finished our coffee. "I'll work on the steps then take him."

I nodded, thinking that would probably boost my son's mood, and reluctantly agreed, making James promise that Connor would be wearing his life vest near the water and to watch him like a hawk. He agreed, and Connor was overjoyed. I knew it would be good for him. Since his father died, Connor hadn't had a male companion except for our neighbor, Mason, who was more like a grandfather, really. That definitely wasn't the same as being a dad.

After James fixed the steps, he and Connor took off. With both kids gone, I found myself with an entire afternoon to myself. I knew I had to be productive, so I decided to start clearing out the outbuilding.

Wearing jeans, an old T-shirt, and sneakers, I took some boxes and garbage bags to the building. I pushed the door open and waved away the dust and musty odors that struck me in the face. I should have left the door open to air the building out before entering. *Too late now*, I thought.

Except for the rocking chair that was moved out, everything else remained where it had been left. I had no idea where to start. My grandparents appeared to be hoarders, keeping newspapers, letters, and books all stuffed into boxes with no rhyme or reason!

I stepped over crates and old chairs to get to the source of light after my eyes noticed sunshine glinting in a far corner. Coming closer, I saw it was a small, wooden rocking horse with sunlight streaming onto it as if it were a spotlight, beckoning an audience. I knew that horse; it was the toy horse my little brother used to rock on. I spotted that horse the first day I came into the building but forgot about it. My brother loved that horse as much as my grandmother loved her rocking chair. *What was it about rocking?*

I knelt beside the toy and placed my hand on the horse's wooden head. Suddenly, the air became cool, and I felt a jolt—like a shock—and closed my eyes.

"Ellie, Ellie, play with me!"

"Not now, Johnny. I'm busy." Busy tanning myself, I thought. But who cared? I needed to look good this summer. Who had time to play with a five-year-old?

"Elise!"

Ugh. I groaned and sat up. Mom had found me.

"Elise, please look after your brother. I need to go into town for some … business."

I squinted my eyes at my mother, noticing she was all dolled up. For what? For a trip into the lame town? Again?

"Where's Gram?"

"She is baking." Mom snapped. "Please look after your brother."

"Fine."

"Ellie, come play!"

I turned to see my little brother sitting in a heap of sand, trying to build something. With a sigh, I pulled myself up from my sunbathing spot and walked over to my brother. It wasn't fair. I was always stuck watching him. Why couldn't he just … go away???

My eyes flew open, and I snatched my hand away from the horse. This damn house and outbuilding continued to bring memories to the surface that were best kept buried. I hated this place. I should never have come back.

I stood up and arched my back to stretch it when I noticed a box sitting near the rocking horse. There was no writing on it, and I was curious as to the contents. Kneeling, I opened a corner of the box and peered inside. It was a box full of kids' stuff—my brother's things. I wasn't sure I was ready to deal with this stuff, but it had to be done at some point. I couldn't avoid the past forever.

I began pulling out the contents: a baseball glove, a baseball, a badminton racket, a box of crayons and several coloring books, and a few small toys and little toy trucks and cars. I wondered why my mother would have kept this stuff, but then I remembered she wasn't the one who packed everything away. My stomach began to tighten as I looked through the items. It was so painful to hold Johnny's things.

I was about to close the box when I spotted something under the toys. Pushing the junk out of the way, I pulled out a blanket—small and blue and very worn. It was my brother's favorite blanket; he dragged it with him everywhere. I lifted the blanket to my face, trying to pull in his scent, but all I could smell was must. I started crying, my face buried in the blanket, and I didn't stop until I was sobbing.

Suddenly, I felt a small hand on my shoulder. I was startled at first, but I realized it must be Connor back from fishing with James. I didn't even hear him come into the building. I was glad he was with me. Connor was such a sensitive child.

I carefully placed the blanket back in the box and turned to hug my son.

No one was there.

I jumped up, my heart racing, and looked around. *"Connor? Connor!!"* I was shouting his name, but he wasn't there. A chill ran through my body. I had to get out of there. I stumbled towards the door, tripping over various items, and finally reached my exit. I yanked the door open and saw a figure standing there. Then I screamed.

Chapter 10

"Ellie? Ellie, hey."

I opened my eyes and found myself lying on a couch. James was kneeling beside me. *What happened? Where was I?* My son was peering around James, clearly concerned.

"What ... where am I?" I tried to sit up, but my head hurt.

"Shh, lay down. You're in the house," James soothed.

The house? Why ... how did I get there? I was in the outbuilding. I heard a scream. Who screamed?

"Mommy? Are you ok? You fell."

I turned when I heard Connor's voice, and pain sliced through my head. "I fell?"

"Ellie, I heard a scream while Connor and I were walking back to the house. We ran to the outbuilding, and you were in the doorway. You must have passed out."

"I ... oh." I touched my head, feeling a lump. *How stupid. Why had I fainted? Something frightened me.*

"Connor, get another ice pack out of the freezer for your mom, ok?" James directed my son, who eagerly ran out of the room to help. Then James turned and looked at me. His eyes were serious, as if he were peering into my soul. I shuddered when he touched my head.

"What were you doing in there? What happened?" James asked softly, stroking my cheek.

"I—I wanted to clean the building out. I found my brother's toys and his blanket—his little blanket. I thought … I heard … " I felt tears falling down my face and turned my head.

"Shh, it's ok, Ell. You have to face this sometime. You've been holding it in for a long time. Years, even."

"I went through a year of therapy, James. I thought I had found peace, but it seems I can't get past it. It's this damn house. There are so many memories here. And … I keep hearing and feeling weird things. I never should have come back."

"Here, Mommy. This will help." Connor came over and placed an ice pack on my head, and I tried to smile.

"Mommy needs to rest now, bud. Why don't you work on a puzzle, and I'll help you in a bit?"

Connor reluctantly walked away, and I closed my eyes. I could feel James sitting there, watching me, but I didn't want to see him. I was still in love with him—that much I knew. But I couldn't talk; I just couldn't. I had enough of talking with a therapist when I was a teenager. I was done.

"Ellie," James whispered. I opened my eyes, and he was leaning toward me. *No, James, no—don't kiss me … don't.*

"Get some rest. We'll talk later." James rubbed my arm and stood up to find Connor. When he walked away, I let out a deep breath. He hadn't kissed me. I wish he had. I closed my eyes and drifted off to sleep.

* * * * *

Morgan returned late in the afternoon, excited about her day out with friends but also exhausted. After a quick supper, she took a shower and then went to her room to nap.

Connor was asleep on the living room floor, where he and James had made a fort, while I rested on the couch. I was feeling better, so I took a mug of decaf coffee out to the porch, along with the dreaded letter I received in the mail, and sat on the swing with a sigh.

Clouds were rolling in, and I figured rain would come soon. That was ok; we needed a little rain. As long as it didn't rain all summer, I was okay with it.

My mind wandered to the incident where I passed out in the outbuilding. I was still perplexed as to why that happened. I remembered feeling a small hand on my shoulder and seeing no one. I remembered seeing someone in the doorway. What was happening to me? Could it be ghosts from the past? But that was silly. There were no such things as ghosts; I knew that. Lately, however, I wasn't so sure.

I sipped my coffee, glancing at the envelope in my lap. With a sigh, I opened it. It was not a long letter; it was just a simple note that said, *I warned you not to go back. The place and its memories need to be torched. They will not let me out of here, or I would do it myself. There are bad things there, bad memories. Do not go back. Let it burn. Let it all die.*

The letter wasn't signed, but I knew who had written it. I was surprised she had written, but they told me she asked for paper and a pencil after she discovered I was back at the lake house. I had no idea what she was talking about, though. The only bad memory was my brother dying, and that was *my* fault. The house needed to be sold, and that was that.

"Hey, Mom."

I looked over as Morgan stepped through the door onto the porch. "Hey, honey. Come sit." I patted the seat next to me, and she sat down, her arms wrapped around her waist like she was cold. She was wearing pajama bottoms and a sweatshirt.

I put my arm around her. "What's up?"

"I'm not too tired anymore. Thought I'd come see what you were up to."

"Just enjoying the evening."

"What's that?" Morgan pointed to the letter on my lap.

"Nothing." I casually folded the letter and stuffed it

under my rear. "Just junk mail."

Morgan just nodded. I was glad she didn't push the issue. We started talking about her day at the beach—what her new friends were like, the volleyball game they had played, going out for ice cream after. I cherished all the time I could get with Morgan and was so happy she was opening up to me. Back home, she was busy with school, hanging out with friends, and drama club. I hoped Connor didn't grow up as fast as Morgan seemed to.

"Hey," she said, looking at me suddenly. "Do you like James?"

I laughed. "Do I like him? Of course I *like* him. We've been friends forever."

I suspected Morgan was rolling her eyes, though I couldn't tell in the dark. "*Mo-om,*" she said, dragging out the word. "I mean LIKE. Do you *like* him? Like … I don't know, love?"

I almost dropped my coffee mug, so I quickly set it on the floor. I looked at my daughter and said as honestly as I could, "Morgan, James and I have a past, that's all. We're just friends. Am I attracted to him? Of course—who wouldn't be? But I only like him as a *friend.*"

Morgan couldn't let it go. "But I've seen the way you guys look at each other. There's this tension, but not, like, *bad* tension. Does that make sense?"

Good Lord, yes, it made sense. She was referring to sexual tension, but I was not about to divulge that information to my fifteen-year-old! Instead, I smiled and stroked her hair. "Honey, there are just things we have to work out. But trust me, no one could replace your dad."

Morgan shrugged and sat back. "I wouldn't mind if you did. James seems cool."

I smiled and looked back at the lake. If she only knew *how* cool.

"James, wait up!" I laughed, nearly tripping over my own feet as I ran to catch up with him.

"Come on, slowpoke!" James grinned at me with that sexy smile

of his, but he kept going. We were going for a hike in the woods, and he was totally teasing me.

"Ok, but if I pass out, it's all on you!" I called out.

As I hurried to catch up, I suddenly heard a small voice behind me, and I groaned. It was my little brother. Why was he tagging along again?

"Ellie, Ellie, wait! Can I come too?"

Johnny was running after us, carrying his trusty walking stick and a small backpack, no doubt carrying some gum and snacks he had found in the kitchen. I tried not to roll my eyes. My little brother was cute but so annoying.

"Hey, buddy," James called out. "You can come with us!"

"James!" I hissed, my eyes wide. "No, he can NOT."

"Ellie, come on. The kid has no one to play with. Just this once. I'll make it worth your while." He ran his fingers over my cheek, and I felt tingles throughout my body.

"Fine," I grumbled. "But this one time! Next time, I want you all to myself."

"Mom?"

"Oh, sorry, honey." I snapped out of my daydream and smiled at my daughter. "Let's go find a snack."

As we walked inside, I couldn't help but remember that I certainly did have James all to myself the next time we saw each other that summer years ago. And little did I know then that it would be the last time my brother would tag along with us.

Chapter 11

I sat on the porch, watching my kids head to the sandy beach. The sun was high in the sky, and the day was perfect. I had a little sunburn from being outside a few days prior, and I didn't want to push my luck. So, despite my anxieties, I allowed Morgan to watch her brother on the beach as long as they didn't go in the water. I told them to play for a bit and when they wanted to go in to let me know and I'd come down. I could see them from the porch anyway, so that made me feel a little better.

I also managed to push the words from my mother's note out of my mind—or, at least, into the back of my mind. It didn't mean anything. Mom was—well, she was in a looney bin, for crying out loud! She was being dramatic at best.

"Hey there."

I jumped at the sound of a man's voice and turned to see James coming around the corner. He was more tanned than when I last saw him and looked absolutely *fantastic* in dark blue shorts and a fitted black shirt. My heart jumped a little, and I silently chastised myself for feeling that way. I did feel a little frumpy in my tan shorts and green short-sleeve shirt that said "Beach Bum" on the front. *How very sexy.*

"Hi! What's going on?" I tried not to show my nervousness. There was nothing to be nervous about. *Just friends. Just friends.*

"Just seeing what you guys were up to. You let the kids go on their own, eh?" He nodded towards the beach.

"Well, yeah, but not in the water. They can't go in the water without me there."

James sat on the swing next to me, our legs almost touching. "Ell, don't you think Morgan is old enough to keep an eye on her brother in the water? Besides, they're right there. You can see them."

I glared at the man sitting next to me. He should know better. James, realizing his mistake in voicing his opinion, held his hands up in mock surrender and laughed. "Ok, ok. I get it."

"Thank you."

I turned my head to watch my kids. Morgan was chasing Connor with a beach ball, and they were both laughing. My heart melted at the sight.

"I was wondering," James started, causing me to turn back to him, "if you wanted to go to the Fourth of July festivities together."

I nodded slowly. That couldn't hurt, could it? We were friends and neighbors, after all, and we were planning on attending anyway. "Sure, we can drive to town together. Connor would like that."

"And you?" James asked with a cheeky grin.

I nudged him playfully. *Was I flirting?* "Perhaps." *Yep—I was flirting all right.*

We sat in companiable silence for a while until Connor yelled that he was ready to get in the water. James and I looked at each other and smiled, and to my surprise, he grabbed my hand and pulled me up from the swing. We stood looking at each other for a few seconds longer than we should have, when my son yelled to me again.

"Go on," James said with a grin. "I'll catch you this

weekend."

I watched James walk away, and when I finally turned around, I saw Morgan looking at me, a knowing smile on her face. Whatever. I didn't care what she thought. I was an adult, and she *did* give her blessing, right?

* * * * *

The next day brought rain. It wasn't just a few drops or light rain. Torrents of rain pelted the windows with such force that you couldn't see out. The kids grumbled at first, but I prodded them into getting a game of Monopoly started while I sat nearby and tried to read a book I had barely gotten into. I couldn't concentrate, though. My thoughts kept going back to the note I received, *warning me* about this place. I shook my head. She was out of her mind—hence the reason she was at the facility she would remain at until she died.

A clap of thunder jolted me out of my thoughts, and I jumped slightly. Lightning flashed outside, and the lights flickered.

"Whoa, that was cool!" Connor shouted, jumping up from his spot on the floor. As he did, his knee hit the Monopoly board, and pieces went flying. I half expected Morgan to shout, but to my surprise, she began to laugh.

"You dolt! Look what you did!" she cried while laughing.

Connor just grinned. "You were winning anyway!"

We all laughed, and I set my book down. I had to grab some candles and matches from the pantry before the lights went out. It was late afternoon—almost evening—but with the storm darkening the sky, the house would not hold any light if we lost power. I wondered if James was home and if he was prepared for the soon-to-be power outage. He was always so responsible, thanks to his upbringing, and seemed to be ready for anything. I smiled at the thought.

Thunder crashed again, a flash of lightning streaked by the window outside, and then it happened: the power went out.

"Well, let's get some candles," I called out to my kids.

"You go. I'm going to my room," Morgan said.

"What? What can you do in the dark?" I was bewildered.

"I have a battery-powered lantern, remember?"

"Oh, yeah. Well, Connor does too. Go on, get your lanterns."

The kids ran off, and I made my way to the kitchen, careful not to trip or bang my legs into anything. I was beginning to feel creeped out downstairs alone. I reached into the box where candles, matches, and lighters were kept. The "traditional" use of candles appealed to me. I lit a few and set them around the kitchen. I was fearful of fires, so I didn't want to put candles in the other room if we weren't going to stay there.

As I was pulling the percolator out of the cupboard to brew some coffee, thinking that coffee, candles, and a good storm would be cozy, the thunder erupted again. A heart-stopping crashing sound followed, but it wasn't thunder. Morgan and Connor screamed from above, and I ran out of the kitchen toward the loft, ramming my leg into a small table as I did. I moaned in pain but limped toward the stairs.

"Morgan! Connor! What happened?" I cried, holding my sore leg.

"We're ok," Connor responded from above.

I rolled my eyes. Why the hell did they scream then? "Ok," I called up. "Why did you scream? Was it the thunder?"

"Yes ... and no," Morgan replied as she hurried down the steps, followed by her brother.

I sat on the chair nearby and rubbed my leg. "Well, what's the 'no' for?"

"Um ... we thought we saw someone outside when the lightning jumped," Connor told me, his eyes wide as saucers. I suppressed a giggle at him saying the lightning "jumped." He was only five, after all.

"Are you sure you saw someone? There are a lot of trees and animals, and... I mean, maybe James?" I stood up quickly, ignoring the pain in my leg, and hurried to one of the windows. Looking out, I could see only rain.

"Well, it could have been a tree or … or something," Morgan suggested.

"Not James, Mommy!" Connor cried. "It was a small person."

I shuddered as a chill coursed through my body. "Where, exactly, did you see this so-called person?"

"Next to the outbuilding," Morgan answered.

I turned to the kids, trying not to shake. I hated being out here alone. "Ok, well, no one is here but us, so it was probably your imagination."

Connor shook his head. "No, Mommy. It was a small person like me. And he was standing in the doorway of that scary building."

I grabbed an oversized poncho from the front closet and pulled on some old boots that I was sure had once belonged to my grandfather. As I pulled the hood over my head, Morgan came rushing over to me.

"You are *not* seriously going out there!" she cried.

"Morgan." I sighed. "I'm a grown woman, and I need to protect my kids. I'm going to see if anyone is out there. If it's a grown person, I need to get them off the property. If it's a child—which I highly doubt—I need to see him or her to safety."

"What if it's an animal, like a bear?" Connor asked.

Good Lord. I hope not! "Then I'll run like heck." At least Connor cracked a smile.

"Stay here," I demanded. I grabbed Connor's baseball bat and headed out the front door.

The rain was coming down harder, and the driveway was slick with mud. I could barely see, but I knew the direction of that blasted outbuilding. I wish I could have just burned it down. Who needed all that junk inside?

A clap of thunder caused me to jump and quicken my

pace. The rain made the air feel cooler, and I shivered as I nearly ran, tryingnot to slip as I did. That's all I needed: a broken leg or arm.

I finally reached the building and noticed the door was slightly ajar. I could have sworn I closed it the last time I was in there. I didn't really want to go inside with just a flashlight and a baseball bat, but what choice did I have? I wanted to make sure nothing—or no one—was inside. I wasn't sure what I'd do if I did see an intruder. Maybe swing the bat like heck and scream?

I pushed the door open slowly and called into the darkness. "Hello?" I called into the darkness.

Everything seemed to be the same since the last time I was inside the building. Morgan and I had hauled some of the old broken furniture out and tossed it in a pile to have a bonfire, and I stacked boxes with old newspapers to one side. The only things left were old toys and boxes from childhood. I didn't want to go through those just yet … or ever.

A rustling sound came from the far corner, so I stepped carefully and quietly to investigate. *Please don't be a rat,* I thought, feeling my stomach roll at the thought. Thankfully, the beam of the flashlight revealed nothing that I wasn't aware of. The rustling sound stopped. What in the world was I doing? *Just turn around; go back to the house where it's safe.*

The room glowed as lightning flashed, creating an ominous scene in the old structure. Satisfied that there didn't seem to be an intruder in the building, I turned to leave.

Suddenly, out of nowhere, a blast of cold air rushed in, and the door slammed shut. *No, no, no!!* I began running to the door but tripped over something—was it my feet?— and dropped the flashlight.

"Shit!" I dropped to my knees to grope for the flashlight, which—my dumb luck—stopped working as soon as it hit the ground. I lost my bearings trying to find it.

"Damn. What the—"

My hand stopped on something. It was the blasted rocking horse that my brother used to play on.

Suddenly, I became furious. Furious because I was out at the lake house. Furious because this building was causing me grief and trouble. Furious at my brother for dying. I couldn't stop the rage inside. I was a hurt woman. I had feelings of anger, guilt, sadness, and pain, and I had to just let it all out.

I stood up and grabbed the wooden horse, then hurled it across the room while I screamed. It felt so good, so I decided to kick everything around me. Memories that had been locked away for years erupted with the same ferocity as my insides. I screamed, kicked, and cried until I had nothing else left inside.

Eventually, the rain let up and the thunder ceased. It was nearly quiet, and eerily so. It was time to get out of there.

I heard another rustling sound, then a crash. I slowly turned my head to the wall towards the far end of the building where boxes were stacked. They weren't stacked anymore—they were tossed over, their insides strewn about the cold floor. I couldn't move. I was shut in a creepy building filled with the past—most of it scattered around caused by my built-up rage.

I crept towards the contents of the spilled boxes and looked at the mess. There were just newspapers and other papers that looked like they could be old bills or something. I wanted to leave, but something scurried over my foot, and I screamed. *Just a mouse... Must be a mouse,* I thought.

I looked down, and with the little light left in that building, I could make out a small stack of envelopes wrapped in string. I picked it up, deciding to bring it with me to the house. I hurried in the direction of the door, but before I could reach for the handle, it swung open.

"Mom?"

"Morgan!" I cried, rushing towards her. "Come on, let's get out of here."

I pushed my daughter out of the doorway and grabbed her hand. We ran towards the house, and I realized I had completely forgotten to shut the door to the outbuilding.

"Mom, wait! The door. Do we need to—"

Before Morgan could say another word, the lightning gave its last performance for the night, along with the crashing of thunder that sounded like God's rage from above, and I heard a *SNAP!*

I turned around to see a tree falling … falling. I didn't realize it was my own screams until my daughter grabbed my arm, pulling me back to the house.

We stood near the back door as the tree crashed onto the top of the outbuilding I hated so much, crushing the roof and probably everything inside. Morgan and I stood trembling, holding each other. Then there was silence.

Chapter 12

"What were you thinking? You could have been hurt … or killed!" James handed me a cup of hot tea as I sat shivering under the blanket he had wrapped over my body after insisting I change out of my wet clothes.

Morgan and I had stood outside of the cottage, holding each other and crying when James pulled up in his truck. He had been worried about us in the storm—especially since the trees around the cottage were ancient—and found us in a state of near shock. My son, thankfully, had listened to his sister's instructions and stayed inside, but he had been—his words—"scared to death" when he heard thunder and our screaming.

I took a sip of the tea, relishing the warm liquid coursing through my body, though, at that point, I would rather have had whiskey to calm my nerves.

"But I wasn't, ok?"

"But you *could have been*. Morgan, too," James argued. He sat next to me, looking intently into my eyes. I looked away.

The storm had stopped, and it was dark outside. James calmed the kids down and then they went upstairs. They were exhausted.

I was exhausted. I was scared. But most of all, I wanted to be alone.

"Look, James," I said, turning my body towards his. I ached from head to toe. "I appreciate you coming over, but we're ok now. I just ... I just want to sleep."

"Ellie, what happened out there?"

I sighed. I didn't want to tell James about my rage—about what I saw and heard and found in that awful building. I wanted to close my eyes and let sleep take over. But it was still early enough that if I went to bed now, I'd be up by three in the morning.

"I ... I wanted to check things out. The kids said they saw something—*someone*—outside, and then ... Then I stumbled across Johnny's rocking horse, and I just lost control."

James reached over and put his arm around me. I felt so safe. I wanted to sink into his arms. I wanted to push him away. I didn't know what I wanted!

"You shouldn't have gone out there alone," James said softly.

"I know, I know."

We sat in silence for a minute until I whispered, "Why did they keep his stuff?"

James was silent. He knew my question didn't require an answer. He just let me go. James was good like that. He knew when to remain silent while I gathered my thoughts. Why he was an editor and not a counselor was beyond me.

"The rocking horse, his baseball and catcher's mitt ... *all of that*. It's sick! I want the building down. I want it burned down or torn to the ground."

"Ok, Ellie, calm down."

I pulled away and set my mug down, looking at James. He looked so concerned—his eyes wide, his hair still damp from the rain earlier. God, he was gorgeous. *Focus*.

"This entire place is nothing but bad memories. And things keep happening. The kids see things and hear things, boxes mysteriously crash—what, to get my attention?"

"Ellie, that's—"

"That's what? Crazy?" I jumped up. "Of course, it's crazy! It's bat-shit crazy!" I was on a roll and began pacing the floor. "Everyone went crazy after Johnny died. My mother first … and look where she is! Then my grandmother—well, she must have lost it a little, and then there's me! We're all crazy!"

James stood up and grabbed my arm to stop me. We stood there face-to-face, like two competitors in a duel, daring the other to make a move.

"You are *not* crazy," James hissed. "You're hurt. You're broken! You obviously never had closure, and you are still holding onto the past!"

"And you had nothing to do with that?" I spat.

James let go of my arm and fell silent. He sighed and shook his head. "I would have taken care of you. I would have loved you … I *did* love you. You're the one who left. You shut me out."

I was tired. I was just so tired. I flopped down on the couch in defeat. "Just go," I whispered.

James sat next to me. "I won't. I won't go, Ellie." He took my face in his hand and gently pulled it so I was looking at him. "You can't push me away again. I … Ellie, I'm still in love with you. I've never stopped." He leaned in, and I didn't pull back. His lips touched mine and I melted into his embrace … his lips … his touch. I'm not sure how long we kissed, but when I pulled back, I realized I never wanted to let him go again. But … there were too many lies. Too many secrets. It was too dangerous to let him back into my life.

"I can't, James. There are things … I can't."

We sat in silence for a few minutes, and then James stood up. "Ell, the building is ruined by that tree. I'll get someone to tear the rest of it down and haul the tree away."

I nodded, unable to look at him or speak, still feeling his soft lips caressing my own.

"Here." James set something on my lap. It was the tied-up bundle of envelopes. "You were holding onto those when I found you. Might want to look at them."

I sat there while James grabbed his jacket and walked out the door.

It felt like he was walking out of my life all over again.

Chapter 13

Fourth of July fell on a Saturday, and the day began with sunshine and a clear sky. I was so thankful the rain let up that weekend.

James, true to his word, had men come over to haul the tree out that fell during the storm. The men said they'd return on Monday to start demolition of the outbuilding. I ignored their request to pull the junk out before demolition to see if anything could be salvaged. I told them everything in there was to be demolished.

After showering, I pulled my hair up into a messy bun and dressed in tan shorts and a blue tank top. I felt young and—for the first time in a while—actually pretty.

"Good morning!" I greeted my kids with a kiss when I entered the kitchen. They were eating cereal and still in their pajamas. "All set for the big day?" I poured a cup of coffee and sat down.

Morgan groaned. "It's early, Mom."

"Sure is, but I promised I'd make a macaroni salad for the big cookout, so I need to get an early start."

I had been in touch with Susan, a local who was usually in charge of these events (though I barely remembered her from sixteen years ago), and she said only two people signed up for macaroni salad, so the more the merrier. That was one thing I had been good at making, thanks to my grandma.

"Can I do the canoe race with my friends?" Morgan asked.

I nearly spit out my coffee. Was she for real? She knew I would say no. I didn't want to upset her, though. Before I could say anything, she piped in her two cents, as teenagers usually do.

"Mom, seriously. We'll be wearing life vests! And there are two in a canoe. I'll be safe, I promise." She was pleading with me not just with her voice but also with her eyes. I glanced over at Connor, who—with milk dripping down his chin—just shrugged his little shoulders.

I heaved a sigh. "I guess it wouldn't hurt ... "

"Yes! Oh, Mom, you're the best!" Morgan hugged me and set her bowl in the sink. With a shriek of joy, she ran off.

I shook my head and sipped my coffee. Connor finished up and left the room, and I was left alone. *When did my kids get so big? Why was Morgan growing up so fast?* Those were the thoughts that ran through my mind, and, once again, I sighed.

The kitchen felt lonely all of a sudden, and I realized I missed having a companion. Greg and I hardly ever saw eye to eye, but we loved each other enough to stay together, and it was nice having a man around the house. I didn't want to think about him, though. I made it on my own this long, so I figured I'd be okay.

I stood up and opened the fridge, pulling out the macaroni noodles I had cooked the night before, along with mayonnaise, hard-boiled eggs, celery, onion powder, and tuna. I double-checked to make sure I had all the ingredients and then began putting it all together while smiling at the memory of my grandmother and me working together in the kitchen for the big Fourth of July cookout. My gram made macaroni salad and deviled eggs every year.

That was her staple at the barbecue events, and everyone loved her cooking. My mom usually contributed baked beans (which *were* pretty good), but she wasn't big on cooking.

When I helped my grandma, she would boil the macaroni and let me mix in the ingredients. She'd laugh when I added a little extra mayonnaise, telling her I didn't like my macaroni dry.

Though I watched my grandma bake and cook throughout the years, I was hardly Betty Crocker. However, I could whip up a few things well enough when I had to. Even a quick homemade macaroni and cheese dish was enough to make my kids happy, thankfully.

"I miss you, Gram," I whispered as I stirred the salad together.

I miss you, Elise.

I whipped my head around, the bowl falling from my hands. Who said that? It was almost a whisper. It didn't sound real, but at the same time, I felt a strange presence.

"Grandma?" I whispered.

Macaroni pooled at my feet, and I realized the salad was ruined, but I was rooted to my spot. The temperature in the room had dropped, but as quickly as I felt it, it lifted. What was going on in the house? Did my grandmother's spirit still linger? No, that was silly. Spirits didn't—

"Mom?"

I jumped at the sound of Morgan's voice, the spoon flying from my hands and mayonnaise spraying everywhere. Morgan was standing in the doorway, wiping mayonnaise off her shirt while looking at me strangely. "What happened to the salad?"

"I, uh … I dropped it," I mumbled. I started the cleanup and hoped I had enough ingredients for a do-over.

"You ok?" Morgan's eyebrows were now raised. Fine— she thought I was looney. Let her.

"Fine," I snapped. Then I took a deep breath. It wasn't Morgan's fault I was turning into a jumpy looney. "I'm sorry, honey. I'm tired. I just need to make a new salad." I forced a smile, and Morgan nodded as she left the room.

Pull it together, Ellie.

* * * * *

"What a gorgeous day!" I exclaimed, sitting on a lawn chair next to Gert and James, a plate full of food in one hand and a beer in the other.

The amount of food at the barbecue was astonishing. There were macaroni and potato salads, at least five different types of sandwich rolls, deli meat and cheese, grilled hot dogs and hamburgers, chicken, baked beans, an assortment of baked pasta dishes, rolls, fruit salad, and watermelon. The dessert tables (there were three) were completely full. I was amazed at the turnout of food. And, of course, I filled my plate as much as I could. Hey, it was summer. Calories didn't count.

My kids were hanging with friends—Connor close by so I could keep an eye on him—and James, Gert, and I were finally sitting down to eat.

Gert took a generous bite of her hamburger, a spot of ketchup remaining near her mouth. "Sure is. After that storm we had, we needed this."

The cookout was in full swing and the park was packed. I knew a lot of the locals from summers past and talked to a few newcomers who were either camping or staying in a motel for the weekend. Everyone was so nice—definitely in vacation mode!

The town really put together a great festival every year to celebrate the Fourth. There were games for kids—adults too—as well as tables set up with cotton candy, chocolate fudge, and lollipops.

Connor had a blast during the kid games—he won first place in the sack race!—and Morgan had a great time canoeing, which was, thankfully, uneventful. James tried to get me to do a ring toss, but the buzz from the beer and the giddiness I felt when I was around him turned me into someone who definitely couldn't toss a ring around a stick. He laughed and pulled me to the next game, most likely enjoying the fact that I had loosened up.

People were spread out on blankets or sitting at picnic tables, while kids ran around on the beach or played tag. It was such a great day. I forgot about everything that had been going on in my mind and at the lake house, and I felt so light and ... well, happy.

James and I hadn't talked about what had happened the night of the storm, but the chemistry between us was so strong that it was a wonder no one else could sense it. Or maybe they did and just didn't say anything. We sat close at the cookout, but not too close. I did notice some knowing looks during the parade that morning when James and I were standing together. Well, I'm sure we gave the locals plenty to talk about.

"Your grandson sure is cute," I told Gert, taking a bite of my hot dog and nodding in the direction of Connor and Max. They were throwing a baseball back and forth. Morgan and her friends were on the beach—in view, of course.

"He's a good boy," Gert replied. "I'm glad his awful mother let him stay with me for the week. I'm hoping I can keep him a bit longer than one week." She was speaking of her daughter-in-law, who was truly a city girl and hated anything to do with the "good old outdoors," preferring posh hotels and spas to this.

"Is Bobby working?" I inquired about Gert's son, Max's father, who was a prominent attorney. I met him a long time ago, but we were a few years apart in age, and I never hung out with him.

Gert nodded, still oblivious to the ketchup on her face. I had to stifle a giggle. "He is. But he'll be up to get Max, so I'll get to spend some time with him as well."

"Let's get Max and Connor together again while he's here," I said, loving the fact that my son had someone else to play with besides his sister. I took a bite of potato salad and sighed. It was absolutely delicious.

"Hey, Mom!" I heard Morgan shout, and I looked over. She was running towards me, clad in her bikini, which I still didn't approve of.

"Hey, baby, what's up?"

"Mom," she said breathlessly. "Can I go with my friends down a little further to play volleyball?"

"Where—"

"Just down that way," Morgan said, pointing to an area almost out of sight from where we were seated.

"Oh, honey, I don't know … " I could barely see the volleyball pit. What if—

"Come on, Ell. We're close by, and there are tons of people here. Morgan won't run off. Let the kid have some fun."

I heard James put his two cents in, and I had to mentally count to ten before I even looked at him. Forcing a smile, I nodded my approval. "Ok, sweetie. Don't run off too far."

"*Yes!!*" Morgan ran off, and I heard James and Gert laughing.

I could have strangled James just then for butting in. I took a sip of my beer and watched Connor and Max play, so I didn't have to speak. I hated that Morgan was growing up and I couldn't watch her every second. I was *that* paranoid mother, for sure. But I had a reason to be. Then again, she had gone to the beach with her friends already, and I hadn't been there. I needed to let go. I sighed, putting the cup of beer back to my lips.

"Ellie," I heard Gert say next to me. "That girl of yours is a knockout. She'll break hearts, for sure. I can't put my finger on it, though."

"What, Gert?" I asked, half listening, trying to enjoy my food. I must have put four different types of salad on my plate!

"Well, she doesn't really look like you, so she must resemble her father. Who did you say he was?"

"Oh," I turned to Gert and James, who was staring at me, eyebrows raised, and responded, "Um, Greg. Greg was her dad. *Is* her dad."

"You don't speak of him much, do you?"

"It's, um … painful."

"Oh, I get that, dear. The kids must miss him as well. But it's good to talk about our loved ones after they're gone."

I wished Gert would shut up. I didn't want to talk about Greg. I set my plate down, suddenly losing my appetite, and looked around, hoping to find something else to talk about.

Gert, however, wasn't finished. "Well, those eyes of hers … such beautiful eyes!"

I rolled my eyes, suppressing the urge to throw my beer at her. Deep breath; she means no harm. Gert was just … Gert. She loved to know things and she loved to tell things.

"She does have a … *familiar* look," James added.

My eyes widened as I swiftly looked at James. What in the world did he mean? My heart began racing, and I told myself it was because of the sun and the beer.

"She is a combination of Greg and me, that's all."

James looked at me and raised his eyebrows. I had to breathe to calm down. I slunk down into my chair and tried to be invisible.

"When did you and Greg meet? I mean, Morgan is fifteen, and you were here just … what was it, sixteen years ago?" Gert put in.

Oh my God; oh my God. Please, stop talking, I thought. I had to think quickly. "Ok, yeah … um, Greg and I met … well, see … we started dating right when school started that year and … heh … one thing led to another … "

James narrowed his eyes and looked almost pissed. *Crap.* I waited for him to say something, but to his credit, he pursed his lips and turned his head away. *Phew.*

"Oh, ok," Gert said. Then, to my horror, she looked up at James and chuckled. "She sort of looks like you, James."

I almost threw up. I whipped my head up at James, and his reaction said it all. He was doing the math in his head; he knew. He must know! What in the world was I going to say?

Chapter 14

"I'm not tired, Mommy."

I smiled as I carried my son inside after a long day. He was *definitely* tired; he nearly passed out before the fireworks were set off. It was after ten at night, and we were all exhausted, but I couldn't wait to put my son to bed so I could sit on the porch.

James had ridden with us to town, so obviously he rode back with us. He hardly said a word after Gert's outburst at the park. I had laughed uncomfortably, and—thankfully—Connor had chosen that moment to (accidentally) whip a ball too hard and fast towards Gert's grandson, which resulted in a bloody nose and a lot of crying. After that, everyone was distracted, and the conversation wasn't brought up again. The rest of the day was spent lounging and talking—mostly Gert talking about the store or gossip from town—and swimming in the lake.

James followed me into the house while I brought Connor in. Morgan was already upstairs getting her pajamas on and probably texting her friends about the day. I was happy that she made friends so easily and was having a good time. I was glad I loosened up today and let her go with her friends—let her be a teenager without being an in-your-face mom. My mom had hardly ever been there for me—as far as personal matters are concerned, anyway—but that didn't mean I had to do the opposite with my own kids by smothering them. Parenting was hard. Especially parenting alone.

After Connor was in bed, I went into the kitchen to pour a glass of wine. I had three beers in the afternoon but felt I needed something stronger to relax me. I decided to bring the bottle with me to the porch.

"Want anything?" I asked James, who was waiting for me in the living room.

"I grabbed a beer while you were upstairs."

I nodded, and we walked outside. The night was warm with a slight breeze, and the lake water could be heard lapping over the rocks. We sat on the porch swing together. It would have been romantic if not for the unbearable tension between us.

We swung back and forth in silence. The moon was bright enough to cast its light onto the water. The water was so still that it didn't even seem real. I sipped my wine and relished the peace.

"Ellie?"

I pulled back to the present when I heard James speak. He was looking at me, and we had stopped swinging. I also realized I had finished my glass of wine. I really must have been in relaxation mode. I reached down and filled my glass.

"Tell me about … What did you do when you left here that summer?"

"What do you mean?" I asked innocently as I took a sip of wine and started the swing moving again. I knew exactly what he meant, but I would not admit it.

"You left after the accident. You all went home. After the funeral, what happened to you? Tell me about your life … what you did."

Oh, good Lord, was he really going into this? I wanted to keep everything to myself—all of my dirty little secrets. James didn't need to know. Did he?

"Well, we went back to normal. I went to school in the fall, and—"

"But your mother went to an institution, right?" James interrupted.

I sighed. If he knew so much, why was he asking? I rolled my eyes, thankful he couldn't see me. "Yes, she did, James. But I lived with my aunt and finished school. There's really nothing else to tell."

James nodded, but before he could say anything, I decided to turn the conversation to other things.

"So, have you seen any of the local gang yet this summer?" I was speaking of a group we used to get together with once in a while during summers at the lake. They were a good bunch—Amy, Claudia, Dan, and Mark—but mostly, James and I kept to ourselves, wanting as much time alone together as possible.

James shook his head. "No, but I heard Amy and Mark are married."

"No!"

James laughed. "Yes! Unlikely couple, don't you think?"

I shook my head and took a drink. "That's for sure. I wonder if any of them have kids," I mused.

James turned to me. "So," he said as he popped the top on another beer. "Morgan."

Damn. Why did I mention kids? "What about her?" I didn't turn to look at James's face. I couldn't.

"I don't know. I mean … her face … she looks a lot like me, don't you think? I was just wondering—"

"What?" I demanded.

James stood up and walked down the steps towards the rocks. He stood there quietly, and I followed, wanting to know what he meant, though part of me knew already. I stumbled over to him and grabbed his arm, forcing him to look at me.

"What if *what?*" I repeated, slightly slurring. *Good Lord, I was buzzed.*

James turned around and stared at me. He looked so deeply into my eyes that I shuddered, feeling that he was looking into my soul—something he always used to do. *Damn him!!*

"You know," is all he said.

"You need to stop this *now*," I hissed. "Morgan is Greg's daughter. Why the hell are you so fixated on her?"

"She's mine, isn't she?"

I froze. No one has ever questioned who Morgan belonged to until we returned to this damned place. My aunt was the only person who knew besides Greg. I took a deep breath and held my head high. "She is Greg's daughter. *He* raised her."

"That doesn't answer my question." James narrowed his eyes and grabbed my arms, pulling me closer. "Tell me, Ellie. Tell me that Morgan is my daughter. The math works! You kept her from me all of these years. TELL ME!"

Tears formed in my eyes, and I shook my head, pulling away from him. I ran towards the porch, stumbling as I went. *This cannot be happening. My entire life is unraveling right before me. The secret I had so carefully kept all of these years ... out in the open!*

"Ellie!"

I heard James call out as I reached the porch, and I spun around. "Go home, James!" I cried. "I will not have you destroy what I've tried so hard to build all these years!"

"What, Ellie? You mean *lies?*" James challenged, coming towards me.

"No, not lies, James. Just reality. We were young. We were *stupid!* My brother DIED because of us, and no one— NO ONE—will know the truth. So leave!!"

"Ellie, this needs to stop. The lying, the secrets—all of it."

"No! I will *not!* No one can know, James. No one! Especially Morgan!" I was crying now.

James reached me and pulled me close, shaking me slightly. "You will tell the truth. She is my daughter and has a right to know."

"James … no." I was shaking from head to toe with anger. How dare he come back into my life and demand anything from me? Morgan would be so upset if she knew. She'd be upset that I kept this secret. Connor would be confused. Everything would change. I didn't want change. For so long, I had been able to keep a quiet little life. No one questioned me. The kids were happy and healthy. Why did I have to come to this stupid house? Why does James have to be here?

I took a deep breath. I had to get control. "We have a life that is just fine—and *has been* fine—without you, and no one needs to know. Not even Morgan."

"Mom?"

Oh, no. I turned my head and saw my daughter standing in the doorway, a shocked expression on her face.

Chapter 15

I stayed in bed longer than usual the next morning. My window showed the sky was cloudy, but that was fine with me; it matched my mood. My head was pounding—probably a mixture of alcohol and stress.

I couldn't believe Morgan had been standing in the doorway listening to James and me argue about who she really belonged to. I hadn't wanted her to find out that way. If I were being honest, I didn't want her to find out at all. I knew I should not have returned to the lake house. It's cursed—has been ever since my brother died.

I hastily got ready after dragging myself out of bed. There was no coffee ready when I walked into the kitchen, which meant Morgan wasn't up yet, or she was angry with me still. I started brewing the coffee while keeping an ear out for movement from upstairs. Finally, I heard feet coming down from the loft. Connor ran into the kitchen, and I heard the front door slam, which had to be Morgan.

"Mommy, can I go outside with Morgan? *Please?*" he begged. He was so cute in his little blue shorts, white T-shirt, and baseball hat that his father bought him before he died. He loved that hat and rarely wore it because he didn't want to get it dirty.

"Honey, did you eat? You need to have breakfast first. Remember, if you want to be a big boy, you need to eat your breakfast!"

Connor huffed impatiently. "I *know*."

"Do you want eggs or pancakes?"

"Nope. Bagel."

"And fruit!" I handed him the fruit basket, and he rolled his eyes. *Good Lord. A teenager in the making?*

"Eat your bagel and *fruit,* and then wait for me. Maybe we can take a walk." I fumbled for a coffee mug. I drank way too much alcohol the night before. *How very responsible of me.*

"I don't *wanna,*" Connor whined. "I'm a big boy, Mom."

Oh, so now it was "Mom" not "Mommy?" When did that start?

"Morgan can watch me," Connor continued, his mouth full of … something. Then I noticed he was scarfing down a banana and toasting a bagel.

I poured my coffee, stepped out to the living room, and looked through the window. I didn't even see Morgan. She better not have gone far. I sat on the couch and savored the coffee entering my system. I guess it didn't hurt that Morgan wanted to be alone for a while to think things over. I just hoped she didn't hate me.

A few minutes later, Connor ran into the living room, wiping crumbs from his shirt. "Done!"

"Gee, that was quick." I took a sip of my coffee, savoring the taste, and smiled at my son. "Let me grab something to eat, then I'll go outside with you."

"Mom, please!"

I never heard Connor beg this much, and my head was pounding. "Fine. But stay where I can see you. And stay away from the water! Do you understand?"

"Yes, I do!" Connor grinned and ran to the hall closet, no doubt grabbing his baseball gear. I watched him run outside and went back into the kitchen to toast a bagel. That's all I had the stomach for.

After I smeared butter on the toasted bagel, I took my plate and coffee to the back porch to watch Connor. The sun was trying to peek through the clouds, and there was a slight breeze. I sat down and closed my eyes, breathing in the summer air. I opened my eyes quickly and started eating so my mind wouldn't drift to the past, as it had been doing since I returned.

Connor tossed his baseball around, and when he became bored, he looked around the grass for bugs. I still didn't see Morgan. She hadn't said much the night she found out—er, *overheard*—that Greg wasn't her father. I tried to explain as she ran away, but I think she was too shocked. James stormed off, and good riddance! How could I love and hate the man at the same time? He infuriated me!

"Mommy, I'm bored."

There it was. I was "Mommy" again. I smiled at my son and stood up. "Ok—let me put my stuff inside, and we'll do something." I wanted to look for Morgan, but I didn't say that to Connor. I had to take deep breaths to calm my heart, which was on the verge of racing in anxiety at not knowing where Morgan was.

Connor and I walked around the property for a while, and I let him balance on the rocks by the water and walk in the shallow end on the other side of the rocks. He seemed to have fun splashing in the water and throwing rocks. I sat on the grass watching him, and when I turned my head, I saw Morgan walking towards us.

"Hi, Morgan!" Connor shouted. "Look at me!" He carefully balanced on a large rock, holding his arms out.

"Hi, sweetie," I greeted tentatively.

Morgan didn't respond. She didn't even sit next to me. I waited. Finally, she spoke. "I cannot believe you let me think Greg was my father all of those years."

"Honey—"

"No! I had the right to know. James is ... he is *so* cool; I could have loved growing up with him!"

"Now you listen here," I said sternly, standing up and facing my daughter. "Greg raised you … and he didn't have to. He *chose* to! You were two when we were married, and he legally adopted you. He loved you so much. You will *not* act disrespectful."

Morgan stood there for a minute, just staring at me. "I loved Dad … er, Greg. I always will. We just never had a connection, you know?"

I sure did. She and Greg butted heads often, but she had been closer to him than she was to me. Or so I had thought.

"I'll always miss him, Mom, but knowing I have a father—my birth father who is *alive*—changes things. Don't you think?"

"Of course it does. I know it does."

"I want to talk to James, though. I want to get to know him now that I know … well, he *is* my father."

I sighed. "Why don't the three of us talk together some evening after Connor goes to bed?" I suggested.

"I'd rather get to know him on my own."

Gee, she was stubborn. "Morgan, please let me ex—"

"Not now. Please. I'm still processing this. How could you lie to my face every day of my life?!" My daughter's beautiful eyes were brimming with tears, and my heart ached.

"I'm so sorry. I never meant for anyone to get hurt."

"But lies *always* hurt. You raised me to believe that. It's true. Is there anything else you're not telling me? Is Connor even Greg's son?"

I drew in a sharp breath. "Now listen, young lady—"

"I'm sorry. I'm too upset to talk. I just want to be alone."

"Ok, I understand. Just please don't go far without telling me."

Morgan shrugged and walked into the house. Connor had come up to me and took my hand. "Are you and sissy fighting?"

"No sweetie, we're not." I forced a smile. "Why don't we go hiking in the woods? Just don't touch any leaves this time!"

Connor laughed and we started off for our hike. Morgan would be fine for a while. She needed to chill.

* * * * *

By the time Monday morning rolled around, Morgan was talking to me a little more but mostly keeping to herself. I was happy to give her space as long as she'd come around eventually. I did understand why she was upset, but I also wanted the chance to explain things to her. I was young when I got pregnant! My brother was gone, my family was torn apart, and I felt alone. I needed to explain that I did the best I could for Morgan. Even if that meant lies had to be told.

Gert picked Morgan up for work bright and early. After breakfast, Connor and I went to the beach and hung out for a while. After eating lunch, Connor went outside to play with his trucks in the dirt, and I decided to—once and for all—look at the stack of envelopes I had found in the outbuilding.

I had just settled into my chair outside when I heard trucks rumbling up the driveway. *What in the world?*

Connor jumped up and ran to the side of the house, and I quickly followed. "Mommy, who are they?" He pointed to the two large trucks driving towards us.

Crap. I forgot I had called to have a local company tear down the outbuilding.

"Hi there," a middle-aged man called out from one of the trucks. Connor waved—my little social butterfly—and walked towards him.

"Hi," I greeted, following my son. "Totally forgot that you guys were coming today. Do I need to do anything?"

"No, ma'am. We'll just tear it down and haul it away. Did you get everything out of there you wanted?"

I shook my head. "It already collapsed. I want

everything hauled away. I don't want to keep any of it."

"Ok, if you're sure. We'll get to it, then. Might want to stay in your backyard and keep this little one away from the area. We'll rope it off just in case."

"Hey, Mister," Connor called out to one of the men. "Be careful the little boy isn't in there when you tear it down." Connor was pointing to the building.

The worker looked curiously at me.

"Connor, what little boy?" I asked.

Connor just shrugged. "I see him outside my window sometimes at night."

I laughed nervously and shook my head. "He has an overactive imagination. There aren't any other kids here. Go ahead with the demolition."

The man nodded but told me they'd make sure no one was inside before wrecking it. I nodded and pulled Connor away.

"*Mom,*" Connor whined. "I want to watch them work!"

"Stay out of their way, honey. It's very dangerous. They have special clothing and helmets. Let them do their job."

"But I wanted to make sure the little—"

"Connor! Enough!" I hissed. I was getting tired of this. I loved my son, but enough was enough. Little boys, strange sounds, and items crashing—good grief.

Connor pouted but ran back to his toy trucks. He told me he was going to construct a building out of sticks and tear it down like the men were currently doing to our outbuilding.

I took one last look behind me. *Good riddance.*

Chapter 16

I was standing at the window, watching a storm roll in. Thick, dark clouds hung together, promising rain. The lake looked dark and foreboding. I shivered at the sight.

It had been days since the outbuilding had been torn down and hauled away, but the memory of that frightful experience during the last storm still clung to me. I shivered, and a small part of me wished I wasn't alone while a storm was coming. Morgan was spending the night with her new friend Rachel—Rachel's grandmother was one of Gert's good friends—and Gert took Connor since her grandson was still with her, so I had the house to myself.

James had texted me a few times, but I hadn't responded. I couldn't bring myself to do that yet. I felt awful for my lies ... for keeping his daughter from him! Sure, I had my reasons—and at the time, those reasons seemed sound and sane—but fifteen years was a long time to keep a father from his child. *Ugh, I was awful.*

I stood by the window, staring out at the worsening weather, when a reflection in the window caught my eye. It looked like a woman was standing behind me. I turned around so fast that I nearly stumbled on my own feet.

No one was there.

"Grandma?" I whispered.

Everything was still. Was she in this house trying to contact me? I wouldn't say I believed in ghosts, but could spirits really come into contact with the living? And … after all those years, *why now?* Maybe, since she died in the house alone her spirit lingered. Maybe she was trying to reach me. That was silly, though. Wasn't it?

I stood still, unsure of what to do, when I felt a gust of air shoot past me. I slowly turned my head, and that's when I spotted the stack of envelopes James had brought in the day the roof of the outbuilding collapsed. What did those letters contain? I figured it was a good time to open them, since I was interrupted when the men came to tear the building down. It also seemed that the spirit—my grandma?—wanted me to read them.

After pouring a glass of wine, I took the envelopes out to the porch to watch the storm. It was less creepy being on the porch than being stuck inside with a ghost—er, *spirit.* The air was slightly cool, which was welcome given the hot days we'd been having.

I took a deep breath and said a little prayer before pulling the string off the stack that sat on my lap. I was never really close to God—I believed He abandoned me the summer I was sixteen—but at that moment, I felt I needed Him for whatever I was going to find in the envelopes.

I took a sip of wine and then pulled the string from the stack. Because it was so old, the thread basically came apart. The envelopes, withered with age, called to me, begging me to open them.

I looked up as the clouds rolled by. "Grandma, do you want me to see what is inside?" I whispered to nothing. A cold chill swept over me, and I shuddered. Grandma was near, even outside; I could feel it. Or maybe it was the impending storm.

I gently pried open the envelope on top without reading the front. Inside was a letter dated September 25th, the year my brother died.

> Dearest June,
>
> I have not heard from you since the funeral. My heart breaks. Not just because I miss you, but because of what happened. I know it was entirely my fault. I know that! I've begged you for forgiveness. I wasn't even allowed to go to his funeral. That broke my heart. You will not return my letters. My dear child, why? I need to hear from you. I need to hear from Ellie. She hasn't returned my letters. Your phone number is not in service. Please!
>
> Love, your mother

What the heck? June was my mother; this letter was written by my grandmother. What letters was she talking about? I have never received a letter *or* a phone call from my grandmother since we left. Confused, I sifted through the rest of the envelopes to see who they were addressed to. June Roberts—several of them—and several to Elise Roberts—me. Why didn't my mother give them to me? RETURN TO SENDER was stamped on every letter. We never moved; why had they been returned? I mean, I moved in with my aunt, but my mail was forwarded. Wasn't it?

How did they all end up here? Had my mother even read any of them? Did my grandmother know my mom was locked up in an institution? I thought they spoke. I know my mom told me that my grandma couldn't make the funeral, but apparently that wasn't true. Why didn't

Grandma show up? Questions raced through my mind, and confusion swirled in my brain. I didn't have answers.

I picked up my wine glass and drained the contents, then went back into the house for another. As I headed back to the porch, a clap of thunder hurled through the air, and I jumped, my wine sloshing over the edge of the glass. I'd have to stay inside. I grabbed my letters from the porch and locked the door behind me, then turned on the lamp next to the couch and closed the curtains. I didn't want to look at the darkness or whatever lurked outside. Goodness, I was becoming a jitterbug.

Settling onto the couch, I opened another letter. It took about half an hour, but I read through all the letters my grandmother had written to my mother. I picked up the last one and was shocked at the contents.

June,

I am not well. I can feel it. I've felt it for some time now, and I am sure I will be with your father soon. And with God. I'll have you know I met with a pastor, and through much talk and praying, I can safely say I am right with my God. He has forgiven me for that day. That awful day! I only need your forgiveness and Ellie's. Why aren't you getting my letters?

James has taken good care of me, but he must leave soon. He has college and a life. He comes up on weekends to look in on me, bless his heart. I haven't left the lake house and I don't intend to until the good Lord calls me home. I asked James to check in once in a while even after I'm gone and look after it in case you or Elise return some day.

I love you. I love Ellie. I loved my grandson, and I am so, so sorry for what happened. I was supposed to be watching him. You asked me to watch him so you could run into town, I think. You were always going to town, though you never told me why, but I could guess. I think about that awful fight you and I had before you left that day ... Well, that doesn't matter now. I don't know if you have forgiven me. But, my sweet June, I love you with all my heart. Please know it was an accident. I will be in Heaven waiting for you to arrive someday. In the meantime, I will take good care of little Johnny for you. He is in God's hands now and soon I will hold him as well.

With all of my heart,

Mom

I was stunned. Thunder continued to rumble in the distance, and lightning flashed across the sky. Many thoughts plunged through my mind. *I thought my grandma was in a nursing home. How long had she remained at the house? Why did Grandma think she was supposed to watch Johnny? I thought I was supposed to watch him. I could swear my mom—on her way out, yet again, that summer—called to me to watch him. That's why I carried tremendous guilt: I was supposed to watch him but ran off, yelling to my grandma that he was playing so she could keep an eye on him. Not that it mattered; Johnny died, no matter whose fault it was.*

The amount of alcohol consumed gave me the courage to read the letters addressed to me from my grandma. My heart hurt so bad knowing that she had tried to reach out to Mom and me. So many wasted years! Why didn't I reach out to her? My aunt had told me she was bad off in the nursing home and then she died. My aunt insisted she was sick and wouldn't even know who I was. I had felt it was best to remember her with happy memories and not see her in the state she was supposedly in. Why had everyone lied??

The letters from my grandma basically said the same— she talked about the accident and forgiveness. She did mention a few times that James had asked about me. I shook my head. Then why didn't … ?

There was one letter left. And the return address was blank.

The lights flickered again as another clap of thunder sounded. I loved a good storm, but being in the middle of nowhere all alone was a little creepy, especially after what happened to the outbuilding. I hurried to light some candles in case the power went out, then I opened the last envelope. The letter inside was typed.

Dear Ellie,

I tried calling you, but your number is out of service. Maybe you changed it. Maybe you moved. I have no idea. Your grandmother doesn't know, either. She has tried to reach you and your mother. I miss you and am worried about you. Please don't shut me out. I want to talk about that day. Please call me or write. I'm at the same address and I'll never change my number. If you won't contact me, at least contact your grandma. She misses you.

Always yours, James

A letter from James. A letter written sixteen years ago that I never received. If I had seen it, would it have changed things? Maybe. Maybe not. I clutched the letter to my chest and began to cry.

Suddenly, the lights went out.

* * * * *

I sat there with only candles to light the room. Outside, the lightning continued to flare, and thunder roared angrily in the sky. That's how *I* felt inside. My heart felt broken all over again. The lies, the secrets—it was too much to bear in my heart. What else had my family kept from me? *You're not innocent either,* a small voice inside my head said.

I stood up, intending on making my way to the kitchen for some water, when I heard a noise. It was coming from inside the house … somewhere. I picked up one of the candles and slowly walked around the first floor, trying not to spook myself with things that were only shadows. Old houses made noise, right?

I heard the sound again; it sounded like someone was crying. There was no one in the house but me. Maybe I was hearing things. Or maybe it was the wine going to my head. Water. I needed water. Water sounded like a good idea, because I was definitely not about to climb up to the loft and look around. I think I was starting to believe in *spooks.*

I walked into the kitchen and set the candle on the table. The crying sound became muffled, but it was still there. My eyes shifted to the basement door. *Oh, no way! Not in daylight did I care for basements, and especially not at night in the middle of nowhere during a storm!* As soon as that thought ran through my head, thunder crashed outside, a breeze whipped through the kitchen, and the candles were snuffed out. Perfect. I was engulfed in darkness.

Secrets.

That one word was whispered through the air. *What in the world?* My body began to tremble as I shuffled to the counter, where I knew I had flashlights in a drawer. I fumbled to pull one out, and as I clicked it on and shined it on the basement door, another word was whispered.

Look.

"Look at what?" I shouted to the empty room. "What do you want me to see?" *I am going crazy; I'm sure of it!!*

The air stilled, and everything was silent. I knew I had to go into the basement. I sure didn't like the idea of it, though.

I put on my brave face, inhaled deeply, and pulled the door open. I took cautious steps into the darkness, my flashlight providing just enough light to protect me from falling down the stairs. Part of my alcohol-induced brain, along with being scared half to death, gave me a picture of me stumbling down the stairs, the flashlight flying out of my hands. Then I started to laugh a little. Yep; I was going crazy.

I reached the bottom and shined the light around the small area. Still nothing but the items I hadn't moved. And the desk. Making my way towards it, I could feel a change in the air, and I shivered. A noise came from above, almost as if the house were groaning with old age—or secrets.

"Gosh, I read way too many books," I said, chuckling.

I reached the desk and looked inside, but there was nothing. I peeked around it and behind it … again, nothing. For whatever reason, I decided to look under the desk where the legs stuck out, and sure enough, there was something wedged underneath one of the legs.

"What in the world … ?" I whispered. It was a book—a small one—and I grabbed it, nearly knocking the desk askew. I took a look at the book and saw it was a journal, and it was old. I carefully opened it and read the inside cover.

It was my mother's journal. And it was dated the last summer when we were at the lake house.

Chapter 17

The next morning, I woke to the sound of birds chirping and sunlight streaming through the slit in the curtain. I sat up groggily, feeling the dire need for coffee and water. My body felt stiff, and as I looked around, I realized I was in the living room. I must have fallen asleep on the couch, but I didn't even remember coming upstairs from the basement. I obviously had—and I apparently drank more wine, as the glass was sitting on the coffee table next to the empty bottle …

And my mother's journal.

A glance at the clock told me it wasn't even six in the morning, but I made a pot of coffee anyway. The journal would have to wait; I wasn't in the mood to read that, especially after reading those shocking letters. I was glad my kids weren't here to see me this way. I was letting the past consume me and I couldn't let that happen; it had to stop.

I showered while the coffee was brewing, washing away the previous night's drama, popped some Tylenol for my pounding head, and then took my coffee-filled mug outside to see if there was any damage from the storm.

All traces of the previous night's storm were gone but for some twigs on the ground and beach sand mussed up.

The water in the lake seemed a bit rough, but that didn't stop the geese and ducks from flying about and dipping in the water.

I stared at the water for a while, mesmerized by the waves and the darkness. Water could be wonderful yet so dangerous—so powerful. My body shuddered and I turned away.

I took a walk around the perimeter of the house, sipping my coffee. I was thinking I'd probably need to plant some flowers and trim some of the bushes before putting the house on the market. The outbuilding was gone, and the workers had flattened the area, so I'd have to plant grass there. Or maybe I could leave it as it was. I'd have to ask James for his opinion.

I mentally made a list of what to get when I went into town later to pick up the kids. It seemed like a good day to dive into some work.

As I looked around the property, I spotted something in the bushes near where the outbuilding once stood. I carefully stepped towards the object, squinting to see better. It was a wooden object of some sort. I couldn't make it out entirely, but I knew it was wooden. As I came closer to the bush, I could see the object better. It was lying on its side, but I had no doubt what it was: my brother's rocking horse—the one that was inside the outbuilding when it collapsed.

No. No, no, no! Why was the horse lying in the bush? It was inside the building when it collapsed! It should have been totaled when the workers tore the building down. We didn't pull it out, and surely the workers didn't touch it! I didn't want it. How could it have gotten out?

I sank to my knees, setting my mug down and pulling the horse towards me. It was still in perfect shape. How had it survived the roof caving in or the men tearing the building down? And why was it here?

"Ell?"

I released my grip on the horse and stood up. James

was walking towards me. *What is he doing here?* I brushed my jeans off, then walked to him. "Hey. What are you doing here?"

James raised his eyebrows. "Stopped over to see if you wanted to talk. You haven't answered my texts. What are *you* doing out here?"

I rubbed my face tiredly. I didn't want to keep this from James, but I also didn't want him to think I was crazy.

"I found this." I gestured towards the horse and James moved closer to get a better look. "It was in the outbuilding when the roof collapsed during the storm. It should have been destroyed when the workers tore the building down!"

"Well, maybe they thought it belonged to Connor," James said, shrugging. He picked up the horse and looked it over.

"What are you doing?"

"Ell, there's nothing wrong with this horse. Don't you want to keep it? You know, something of Johnny's to remember him by?"

"No!" I cried, then I stormed away from James and that blasted toy.

When I reached the house, I stomped up the steps and into the kitchen to get some more coffee. *Damn—I left my mug outside.*

I poured two cups of coffee and brought them out to the porch, knowing James would be right behind me. Sure enough, James was sitting on the steps, the rocking horse on the ground at his feet. I handed him a cup and sat next to him.

I stared at the horse, remembering how excited Johnny was to have it. *"Mommy, look at me! I'm a cowboy!"* He rocked back and forth on the horse, whooping and swinging his arm as if he held a lasso. We had laughed and watched as he rocked. He had been a happy child.

James broke the silence and pulled me back to the present. "Ellie, I think we need to talk about Morgan."

I sighed and watched the lake. The water seemed calm

now. Why did everything seem calm when James was around? Maybe *my* inner turmoil stirred everything up around me.

"I know. She wants to spend time with you … get to know you." I carefully stayed away from the fact that I had kept Morgan from James for her entire life. Maybe he wouldn't bring it up. I was so ashamed.

James nodded and sipped his coffee. The sound of mourning doves soothed me, and I closed my eyes, soaking in the sun that was beating down on me. I'd have to put shorts on soon; it was getting warm.

"I can't believe I have a daughter," James whispered. His remark was delivered so quietly that I almost missed it.

My heart ached for him and for Morgan. I had kept a secret from two people I loved, and it hurt. I was an awful person. At least Greg had been a really good father to both kids, even though Morgan wasn't his flesh and blood. He loved her as soon as he met her.

"I'm so sorry, James." It was all I could think to say.

He looked over and put his arm around me. "I forgive you, Ell. I had some time to think about it and … well, given the circumstances at the time, I get why you kept her from me. Though I can't believe fifteen years went by without you telling me." James rubbed his face; he looked tired. "But holding onto anger or regret won't do any good. I want to move forward. I want to have a part in her life. I deserve that."

I only nodded. I also thought it was a good time to tell James something else. "James, I read some letters last night."

"Oh yeah?"

I sat up straight, staring ahead. A goose swooped down into the water then flew right back up into the air. I smiled at its antics. Ahh, to be as free as a goose; no worries except when he would catch his next fish. "Well, there were letters from my grandmother to my mom and then some to me."

"*Ohh,* I think I know those letters."

"You do?" I looked at James in surprise. "They were all sent back. I never saw one of them. Why would my mother or aunt have returned them?"

James heaved a sigh. "Ellie, all I know is your grandma was devastated with each returned letter. Day after day, she waited for a call from you or your mom."

"Mom must have changed our number without telling me," I mumbled. "Wait—why didn't she have someone drive out to us? Why didn't you drive out to find me if you were wondering where I was?"

"Whoa, Ellie. Listen. You know your grandma was too old to drive. And why would she ask someone—and pay them—to drive her to see you and your mom when you two didn't answer calls or letters?"

"But—"

"It was a six-hour drive to your house, Ell."

"What about you?" I asked softly. I always wondered, after leaving the lake house, if James would come after me. He never did.

James rubbed his face again. "I wanted to follow you so bad. I really did." He stared out at the lake, lost in thought. How time had matured his facial features. We had both aged, but not only in years. "My parents loved you, you know. But they insisted I give you time. I mean, your brother just died. They didn't know about us and that day. Of course they didn't. They simply told me to give you time. And I ... I never even thought about the possibility of a baby. I was eighteen! I'm so sorry, Ellie."

My heart softened and I placed my hand on his. My thoughts turned back to the day we returned from the lake house.

"My aunt—Mom's sister—planned the funeral for Johnny," I began. "My mother went through the motions, but she was adamant that Grandma not come. I had no idea why! After about two weeks, my mother had a nervous breakdown, and the doctors put her in a 'facility' as they called it, but I call it an institution. That's what they are, right?" I took a deep breath, staring at the water, my mind far away. The silly goose stopped diving and was now floating peacefully in the lake. "She never recovered, James. I stopped visiting after the third time. She just didn't talk to anyone."

"I'm so sorry."

"The doctor once told me the only words she would mutter were something about it being her fault. I imagine she's talking about the accident." I looked at James. "How could it be *her* fault? She left for town that day! I thought it was *my* fault but then Grandma's letter says *she* was supposed to be watching him. Whose fault was it?"

"Why do you need to know? After all these years, why?"

"Because," I huffed. "I was fine before I came back up here. I thought I had laid everything to rest, kept it in the past. Moved on!! But now, being up here ... it's just coming back and it's painful."

"I know. I'm sure it is, but your grandmother is gone, your mother is put away, and you need to leave it all alone. Grieving is one thing; grabbing back onto the past is another. Please, Ell, let it go for the kids, for yourself ... for *us*."

I stared into his eyes like I did all those years ago, feeling trust and love and ... hope. "Is there an *us? Can* there be an us again? After the lies, the secrets ... all of it?"

"If you want there to be. *I* want there to be. We can start over." He reached for me and pulled me close.

James and I sat there—his arm around me and my head on his shoulder—watching birds fly about, singing their songs, the water lapping up to shore, and the warm air enclosing us.

I finally had to pull away. "I need to pick the kids up." I stood up to go inside and change.

"I'm going with you. We can get lunch together."

"I don't know ... "

"I'm going."

I nodded. James was stubborn but I was glad for it this time. As I was walking through the door, another thought hit me, and I turned to James.

"Will you take me to the cemetery where Grandma was buried? I'd like to visit her grave and bring her flowers."

James looked confused. "I have no idea where she's buried. I left after securing the house for the winter. Charlie told me he found her will on the table, and he'd take it into town and take care of everything."

My heart began to thump loudly. Where was Grandma buried? Surely, she must be in the town cemetery. James just didn't know. I'd figure it out. I couldn't think about that; I had to change and get the kids.

I hurried to get ready—trying to look somewhat pretty for James—and fifteen minutes later, we were headed to town.

James and I picked up Connor at Gert's and stopped at Rachel's house to grab Morgan. I had to put my grandma out of my mind for the afternoon so I could function.

The girls were sitting outside looking at their phones when we pulled into the driveway. Rachel waved as Morgan said goodbye and trotted to the car. She slowed when she saw James but gave him a tentative smile.

"Hey, honey." I pulled Morgan into a hug and opened the back door for her. She climbed in and playfully punched Connor in the arm. "Did you have a nice time?"

"Yeah, we stayed up late watching movies. Oh, and we made s'mores in the fire pit. It was cool."

"I want s'mores!" Connor shouted.

"We can make some back at our house, butthead," Morgan shot back jokingly.

I rolled my eyes. "You're probably tired, but James and I thought we'd take you and Connor to lunch."

James turned to Morgan and smiled, and she smiled back shyly. *So far, so good.* I pulled away from Rachel's house and followed James's directions to a restaurant near the water. I vaguely remembered the place, probably because my mom rarely took Johnny and I anywhere nice to eat. We usually ate our meals at the lake house or a diner in town. Grandma was an excellent cook, but it was fun to go out to eat once in a while.

We piled out of the car and walked towards the restaurant like a real family. Connor grabbed James's hand as we walked through the parking lot, and my heart melted a little. I smoothed out my pale-yellow sundress and took in the scene.

The restaurant was a large wooden structure situated adjacent to the lake, with a patio facing the water. Several tables with umbrellas were scattered about the patio. There weren't many people out yet.

The waitress seated us at a table on the patio and Connor was thrilled to have a view of the lake. After ordering drinks—Sangria for me, beer for James, and lemonade for the kids—we sat back and looked at the menu.

"Morgan, do you like seafood?" James asked, setting his menu down.

Morgan shrugged. Her hair was pulled back into a ponytail, and it looked like her arms got some sun. She looked young, like her own age. "I think I like *some* things. I haven't really tried much."

"I'll have to grill up some salmon and haddock someday. I think you'd like it. You too, buddy." James tousled Connor's hair.

Connor looked positively thrilled to have a man giving him attention. I was sure he got sick of his sister and me from time to time. Boys needed father figures.

"I'm going for the chicken sandwich," I said, closing my menu. "What are you getting, honey?" I looked at Connor who was studying the menu. He could read well enough for his age, but some of the menu items were difficult for him.

"Maybe a burger?" he asked, scrunching his nose.

James helped Connor with his order, and we sat

chatting while we waited for our food.

"You kids ready to get back to school in the fall?" James asked.

Morgan shook her head and Connor grinned and said, "Yes! I love school. I have so many friends. This year I probably will play soccer … " On and on he went, telling James everything he planned on doing once school began.

Morgan finally got a word in. "I'm not crazy about school, but I love English. It's my favorite subject."

James grinned as he took a sip of beer. "That was my favorite subject, too."

Morgan smiled. "Really? That's cool! I don't like reading much when I'm on vacation," she said, giving me a pointed look, "but I like the books the school suggests for us, especially the classics."

"I enjoy classics as well," James said.

"Charles Dickens," both James and Morgan said at once. We all laughed. It was almost too good to be true how well they were getting along and how much they had in common.

James and Morgan began talking about their favorite books and essays they had written in their English classes. I sat back happily, sipping my Sangria and enjoying the time with my kids—and James—while looking at the lake. There were many boats out, and a few jet skis. I loved seeing the lake busy this time of year. When I was a teenager, I wanted to learn to drive a jet ski, but my mother didn't have the time to take me to lessons. That's what she told me, anyway. I felt I missed a lot back then because of the absence of my parents.

Our food arrived and we ate in companiable silence until Connor remembered a funny story involving his friends and French fries. He chattered on, and I watched as people walked along the beach below us. Soon, more people were seated on the patio; the laughter from others and chatter was a nice sound. It was such a lovely afternoon. I didn't think anything could ruin it.

"Mom, have you ever been on a canoe?"

I turned to Morgan who had a sly smile on her face. Oh, dear. "Um, yes, actually. But I don't like boats much anymore," I mumbled.

"Well, Rachel said there is a place here where we can rent one. Can we?"

"Yeah, Mom, can we?" Connor chimed in.

"Gee, I don't know … " My heart began to race and my hand shook.

"Mom, I was out on the canoe at the Fourth of July picnic, remember? The race?" Morgan begged.

James, who was sitting next to me, gently placed his hand over mine. "I happen to own a canoe. Would you two like to go out on the water with me?"

I turned to James with a frantic look. *No, no, no!* He was not taking my kids on the water! *Please, not that.* It was bad enough I had to suffer through Morgan on a canoe with her friends, but *Connor* out there? He was a beginner swimmer! My heart was racing.

"Mom, *can we?*" Morgan sounded so excited, and I *did* want her to get to know James—er, her *father*.

"Ellie, trust me," James whispered. I turned to him as he squeezed my hand, his eyes boring into mine. *Damn those eyes.*

"Ok," I whispered back, my voice shaking.

James grinned, and I noticed Morgan had a knowing smile. Connor pumped his fist into the air and cheered. The kids talked excitedly with James about their upcoming canoe adventure while we finished our lunch. With my appetite mostly gone at that point, I just nibbled on some fries.

When we left, Connor grabbed my hand and James's hand, while Morgan walked next to me, holding my arm.

As we walked through the parking lot towards the car, we passed another couple, older than James and me— maybe my mom's age? The man looked familiar, and I couldn't help but stare. He stared back.

"Ell?" James asked.

I shook my head and both the man, and I looked away. "I'm ok," I said, almost whispering. As we walked to the car, I had an awful feeling in the pit of my stomach.

That man. He looked like ... well, he looked like my brother.

Chapter 18

The next day, James brought his canoe over and tied it to our dock. I made sure the kids had their life vests fastened and gave them the lecture about not leaning out of the canoe and making sure they listened to any instructions James gave them. I was a nervous wreck, but it was a beautiful, sunny day—we had gotten lucky over the summer with more sunny days than not—and I wanted the kids to enjoy themselves.

"Ok, guys, you ready?" James helped Connor into the canoe and Morgan followed.

I stood on the dock watching the man I loved in a tiny boat with my children. "James, take care of my babies," I said. I anxiously pushed away thoughts of my brother drowning all those years ago. Was I overreacting—being dramatic, as Morgan would say? Probably.

"We'll be fine, Ellie." James winked at me, and I took a deep breath.

"I'm not a baby, Mom!" Connor shouted and we all laughed.

I waved as they set off over the water, then walked back to the house. I had some cleaning and sorting to do, and I figured it was a good time to do it since it would keep me distracted. I had also put the image of the man I saw the day before at lunch out of my mind. It had to be a coincidence that the man in the parking lot resembled my brother. After all, my mom only had two children, and one was dead.

I grabbed boxes to collect items we didn't want. When my grandmother died, her stuff was left except for what James threw out—the obvious things like food that would go bad—but most of the stuff remained. Since the outbuilding was taken care of, I only needed to weed out the inside of the house.

I went up to the loft, but there wasn't much to clear out since the rooms had been empty except for what we brought for the summer. I stood up there looking around, remembering my days sleeping in the loft. I used to set a blanket by the window and read while occasionally looking out at the lake. There had been a lot of peaceful times up here when I was growing up.

I left the loft and tackled the downstairs room where I was sleeping. There were a lot of knickknacks, old paintings on the walls, and clothes that Grandma left behind. I boxed everything to donate to the Salvation Army.

The living room furniture could stay, but I went through the books in case there was anything I wanted. Some mystery novels, a Bible, and some books on gardening were the only things on the shelf. I kept the Bible and placed the other books in the box for Goodwill. I spotted my mother's journal still sitting on the coffee table, but I knew that would have to wait.

By the time I finished boxing things up, I figured it was time to make lunch since the kids and James would be returning soon.

I hurried to the kitchen and made a platter of sandwiches then pulled bags of chips from the cupboard and fresh lemonade from the fridge. As soon as everything was set out, I heard a door open and my son's voice call out.

"Mommy, that was so much fun!" Connor ran into the kitchen and threw himself at me. I embraced him and started to catch onto his excitement. I silently said a "thank you" to God for bringing my kids back safely to me.

"Honey, tell me about it!"

"Mom, James is a great driver—I mean paddler," he laughed a little.

Morgan and James came in, chatting happily. I loved the sight. It also frightened me. Could we really be a family? Could the past be buried—once again—and we truly become a happy family?

"Mom, I'm starving!" Morgan exclaimed, snapping me out of my thoughts.

"Oh, sorry, honey. I made lunch."

We sat around the table eating while the kids talked about their day. I was happy that they had a good day and were brought back safely, but I was itching to read my mother's journal. I had been so busy packing things up, I hadn't gotten a chance to look at the journal yet.

Finally, two hours later, that time came. James had gone home, and the kids were showered and lounging in the living room. I took the journal out to the porch so I could read in privacy while it was still light out.

June 28

The kids and I are settled at the lake house. Mother is doting on them, of course, though Elise is "too old" to be doted on. She's growing up so fast, it frightens me. She and James are bound to spend more time together this summer. They do every summer. I love James like a son, but he's older than my Ellie, and I'm afraid ... well, it doesn't matter. She's old enough for a crush, but she's not stupid. She wouldn't do anything foolish.

Me, on the other hand ... I see Sam every time we're here for the summer, but I feel my mother is getting suspicious. She's even asked about him a few times, which is normal *since they were friends before he and I ever ... got together. Sam was always good to Mom, and I feel bad about what happened between us, but I can't take it back. I just have to keep hiding the secret and hope my mother doesn't get wise. Johnny is growing up fast and he looks more like his father every day.*

What in the world did my mother mean by that? Who the hell was Sam? Why did she have to sneak out? Did my mother have an affair?

* * * * *

I tossed and turned in bed that night, unable to sleep. A nice breeze was floating through my window, but my mind was tormented by the journal entries I had read so far. I had only read three of them but had to put it down for the night; I couldn't read further.

My mother had kept her own secrets that summer. She didn't mention Sam in the few entries I read after the first one but talked about Johnny and how he would grow up without a father, stuff like that. I assumed that was because my father had died when Johnny was young. But was she talking about Sam? Was *Sam* Johnny's father? And if so, why would Johnny grow up without a father? Was Johnny really my half-brother? Was that the reason my mother went to town so often when we were up here each summer? I felt sick. I wondered if anyone else knew about it.

Sleep finally claimed me, and I dreamed of beaches and happy families—none of them mine.

* * * * *

Monday rolled around, and since Morgan would be working all day, I thought I'd do something fun with Connor—maybe drive up to Eagle's Peak and take a hike up the mountain. It wasn't a tall mountain, more like hiking uphill, but I knew Connor would love it. James and I had climbed that mountain a few times during the summers we had come up here.

I stayed in bed for a few minutes thinking about the fun James and I used to have on our mountain hikes—finding interesting plants and funny-looking trees, making it to the top and screaming like Tarzan. It would be fun to watch Connor experience that as well. Well ... maybe I wouldn't scream like Tarzan this time.

I slipped my robe on and padded into the kitchen to get coffee, not even bothering to change out of my pajamas. I took my mug outside and sat down, listening to the birds talking to one another. The lake was still, and the sun was already bright in the sky. Another beautiful day at the lake. Why was my heart so heavy, then? Oh, right—my mother may have had an affair, and Johnny is probably not my dad's kid.

I sipped my coffee and rocked on the swing, still upset after reading about my mother's affair. It was clear that she *had* been having one, and the more I thought about it, the more it made sense. My father—when he was alive—was always busy with work; he worked late hours and often didn't have time for any of us. In fact, he hardly ever came up to the lake house. It was a six-hour drive, and by the time the weekends rolled around, Dad claimed to be too tired after working sixty hours a week. That caused a rift between him and my grandparents, and, of course, my mother. Still, that wasn't an excuse for my mother to find comfort in another man, but it explained *why*, I guess.

"Morning, Mommy," I heard a little voice say.

I turned with a smile as Connor sleepily slipped out the door and walked over to me. I moved over for him to sit down, and he snuggled against me. We rocked for a bit. It was nice, the two of us having some cuddling time and enjoying the quiet morning. and then Connor seemed to wake up fully.

"What are we going to do today?" he asked with eagerness in his voice.

"Hmm, well, Morgan has to work, so what if you and I hiked up a small mountain?"

Connor sat up and gave me a grin, his eyes wide. "That would be amazing! What should I wear?"

I laughed and patted his head. "Well, first, how about we get breakfast?"

"Ok, ok," he grumbled. "Cereal because it's faster!"

Connor ran inside to get breakfast and I followed. It was time to start the day, not brood over my family's past. That could come later.

* * * * *

Connor and I had a great day hiking. I pointed out different leaves and trees to him, and he gathered as many "cool" twigs and rocks as he could carry. My son sure did love the outdoors.

While we were hiking, we came across some really neat-looking stones sticking up from the ground, and my mind jolted, remembering that I still didn't know where my grandmother was buried. I vowed to make sure to find out soon.

After our hike, Connor wanted to go swimming, of course, but I talked him into getting ice cream in town first. I just had to ask someone about Grandma's grave!

We got into town, and Connor waved to almost every passerby he saw. His enthusiasm was contagious, and I found myself greeting people as well.

The ice cream shop was packed, and after ten minutes, we came out with a small, soft ice cream cone with rainbow sprinkles, then I hurried Connor over to Gert's store, ordering him to sit on the bench outside and wait for me.

I entered the store and saw Morgan happily chatting with an older customer. I gave her a quick smile and wave, then went to the counter where Gert was counting change.

"Ellie! What a nice surprise!" Gert set her change down and smiled at me. "Everything ok?"

"Gert, can we talk privately?" I asked, nodding in

Morgan's direction.

"Sure, hon." Gert's brows were furrowed but she motioned to the back office.

"Connor is outside; can we talk there?"

"Of course."

Once Gert and I were outside, and I felt we were far enough from Connor's little ears, I plunged in. "Gert, where was Grandma buried?"

"Oh! Oh, um. Oh, dear." Gert was wringing her hands and looked incredibly uncomfortable.

"Gert!"

"Dear, I thought you knew!"

"Knew what? I didn't even know she died in the lake house! Why is everything a secret? Please. I need to know!"

Gert took a deep breath. "Honey, she … well, her will specifically instructed that she be buried on the land at the house."

My heart stopped beating; I was sure of it. I felt dizzy and nauseous. "She … what?"

"She was buried near the rock edge by the water. Charlie and a few others did it secretly because … well, you know, it's illegal, really. Isn't it?"

"Mommy, all done!"

"Ellie, are you ok, dear?"

I heard her voice but my vision was blurry. I had to sit. Where was the bench? Voices continued around me, and I felt someone take my arm and lead me to the bench. I sat down, leaned over, and placed my head between my legs, breathing deeply.

"Let me get you help."

I heard Gert's voice but couldn't lift my head. I felt Connor's hand on my back; I couldn't move. My grandmother's body was buried on our property. She wanted it! Why? That was sick!

I finally took enough deep breaths and was able to sit up. Connor, with sticky ice cream on his face and hands, along with a few people I didn't know, were standing around me with concerned looks. I forced a smile and stood up.

"Elise! Are you ok?"

I turned to see our mailman, Ronnie, hurry to me.

"I … I think I am, Ronnie. I'm ok."

The others slowly walked away, giving me odd looks and murmuring things, and Connor took my hand. I had to get home. I couldn't break down here.

"Let me take you home, sweetie," Ronnie said softly. "You can get your car tomorrow."

I nodded mutely. Gert came back into view and took my son's hand.

"I'm taking Connor and will bring him home with Morgan later. I could use some help from a big boy!" Gert gushed, trying to put on a brave face of her own for my son.

They hurried into the store, and I followed Ronnie to his truck. We didn't speak the entire way back to my house. Ronnie helped me out of the car, and I waved to him as he backed out.

What now?

* * * * *

James found me sitting on the ground near the water—close to the rock edge, but not too close. I had no idea where Grandma was buried and the last thing I wanted to do was sit on … *her.*

"Are you ok?"

I turned to James, my eyes wide. "Am I ok? No, I am not ok! Did you know about this?" I waved my arm around the grassy area.

James plopped down next to me and pulled his knees up to his chest. "I had no idea, Ell. I told you that."

"It's sick. It's … Why in the world would she want to be buried here?!"

"Maybe you should look at her will. Ask Charlie, or call the lawyer … um, Tom, I think his name is. There has to be a good reason," James suggested.

"Yeah," I muttered. "She didn't want to leave because she carried guilt over Johnny. I bet that's why."

James and I sat there for a while in silence. I was trying to process everything, but my heart was so heavy. I sighed heavily, putting my head in my hands. Maybe I overreacted over the whole thing. That was me. Elise, the Overreactor.

At last, James spoke. "Maybe we should have her moved to a cemetery."

I nodded. "I guess. At some point."

"The kids will be home soon. You better clean up," James told me, standing and holding his hand out.

I took his hand, and he pulled me up. We stood there gazing into each other's eyes, and then James gently pulled me away from the water and towards the house. I didn't glance back.

Chapter 19

The summer seemed to be moving along. It was nearing the end of July, and I felt like the kids and I made much progress on the house. We planted flowers alongside the back porch where the sun shone the most during the day. Connor helped to haul rocks back where they belonged by the water's edge, carefully placing each one as if he were constructing a building. I still didn't know exactly where Grandma was buried, but I tried to push that thought away from my mind every time it snuck up. I could figure that out when we left at the end of summer.

Morgan and James spent one-on-one time together as well. They would go for walks, meet for lunch when Morgan was working at the store, and text often. I loved seeing Morgan with James—beautiful moments where they were getting to know one another—yet the guilt at keeping them apart for fifteen years was eating away at me. I was also scared. What would happen when we left at the end of the summer? I hadn't planned on keeping the cottage—James knew that. He also knew we'd be heading back home. And it occurred to me that I didn't even know where his permanent home was.

On a balmy Friday evening, Connor was playing with his trucks, and James and I were sitting on the porch with after-dinner wine. We had grilled fish that James had caught, though Connor ate a hot dog instead, stating fish was "yucky."

"Have you read any more journal entries?" James asked as we watched Connor shove dirt into the back of one of his dump trucks. I wondered if he'd be in construction when he was older. He sure did love trucks and building things. Johnny had loved his trucks, too.

"I haven't had time, and when I do sit and relax at night, I'm either too tired to read or forget it's there."

James nodded, lost in thought, then casually put his arm around me. I felt warm all over and suppressed a shudder.

Just then, it occurred to me that James knew pretty much everyone in town. Maybe *he'd* know who Sam was.

"James, did you know anyone named Sam in town? You spent every summer here, even years after we left."

"Sure. Sam Davis had a farm a few miles out of town and sold goods at the farmer's markets every summer. He was a great guy. Surprised you never heard of him."

"Me, too. Especially since Gram and Gramps seemed to know everyone around here." I sat there lost in thought. My grandparents spent every summer here, but they would come up in the fall and spring to check on things. Even if Sam Davis lived outside of town, they'd have heard of him or met him. Mom's journal seemed to indicate they had been friends. *Maybe I'd have to ask Gert,* I thought.

"Do you know how old he might be?"

"I'd say maybe mid-sixties. Why?"

Crap. That couldn't be the Sam my mom wrote about. He would be about ten years older than my mother. I mean, I guess he could be the same Sam.

"Oh, wait!" James said suddenly.

"What?"

"Sam was the guy we saw in the parking lot when we left after lunch with the kids. You looked right at him!"

The man who looked like my brother.

"You ok, Ell?"

"I ... yes, I'm fine." I smiled at James, though I knew it didn't reach my eyes. I was sure James wasn't fooled but he didn't say anything.

"James, look what I built!" Connor shouted.

James pulled away from me and, after giving me a quick side-glance, walked over to inspect Connor's creation.

I was distracted for the rest of the evening but managed to tuck Connor into bed later and make my way back to James, who was still on the porch. I sat next to him, and we swung in silence for a few minutes.

"Ell, what's going to happen at the end of summer?"

"What do you mean?" I knew exactly what he meant but pretended not to. Instead, I stared at my wine glass and fiddled with a loose string from my sweater. I really needed to buy new clothes for myself. I was like my mother in that way—I'd buy new clothes for the kids but hardly ever for myself.

"You know what I mean. You'll leave here and take the kids back to your home, they'll resume school, and I'll go back home. Then ... will I see you? Will I get to see Morgan?"

I shook my head slowly, not having an answer. James wasn't going to let it go, though. He stood up and began pacing. I watched him as he did, recalling that nervous habit of his.

"I want to have a relationship with my daughter. And you and Connor also. How can we do that?"

"James, I don't know. Things have been so ... I don't know. Do you really think we can start over? After my lies and—"

"*What?* After all we've been through? We have a child together! We've had so much fun together this summer. I thought ... "

I set my wine glass down and stood up, facing the man I knew I would always love. I wanted nothing more than to pull him close and kiss him when he looked at me with those intense eyes. But I couldn't. I didn't know why I was holding back my feelings for him. I was a grown woman, after all, and my feelings mattered. I didn't know why I couldn't let myself go. My kids would grow up some day and move on and I'd be left … well, alone.

I shook my thoughts away and came back to the present. "James, look. I held onto that secret for a long time and I carry that guilt. There are things you don't know about me. There are things I am learning about my family and the past. You don't want to be involved in that."

"Why don't you let *me* decide what I do or do not want?" His beautiful eyes flared with anger, and he stormed off the porch and headed to his truck.

I walked down to the water's edge, sat down, and cried. I was coming undone; I could feel it. I was fine until I returned to the lake house. Now everything was falling apart. Again.

"So, Elise. Tell me about last week, after you left here."

I fidgeted in my seat. I had been making progress, hadn't I? Why bring up the past … which was last week?

My therapist waited patiently, and I finally spoke. "Well, um, I did ok."

"Until … ?"

I looked down at my hands. "Until I saw a little boy at the gas station who looked like Johnny." I said it almost in a whisper. It was a wonder my therapist heard me at all.

"Elise, you're going to have those moments. It's ok to feel sad and to cry when people you love pass away."

I looked up at her in disbelief. "I completely came undone!"

"It was a trigger," she said in a reassuring tone. "Just a trigger. And you handled it, didn't you?"

"Sure, but how many more of these triggers am I going to have in my lifetime?" I challenged.

"I don't know, but at least we can work on how you handle it

when it happens. What do you say?"

I snapped back to the present and looked out at the beautiful lake before me. The lake was calming; it was settling for me. Unlike my inner turmoil.

Years ago, my therapist taught me how to handle "triggers" when they happened, and I had managed them all my life up until returning to the lake house. I couldn't let my children see me this way. I couldn't—and didn't want to—let *James* see me this way. I had to take deep calming breaths and write down everything I was thinking and going through. Otherwise, I'd unravel into the person I became when I left the lake house all those years ago. I didn't want to end up like my mother.

Chapter 20

"Mommy, where's Morgan?"

I turned from the coffee maker to see my son rubbing his sleepy eyes as he walked into the kitchen. It was a humid morning—already nearing eighty degrees—and my guess was that Connor couldn't sleep anymore. It *was* pretty hot upstairs, even with fans. The house was so old I didn't want to risk putting in an air conditioner, so fans had to do.

"Morning, honey." I leaned down to give him a hug and a kiss. "Morgan left early to spend the day with friends hiking." I thought it would be too hot to hike, but Morgan insisted she'd be fine. I made her bring extra bottles of cold water, just in case.

I sat at the table with my mug of coffee and checked my phone. No messages. I hated that service was spotty in the middle of nowhere; partly in case of an emergency but partly because I was hoping James would text me. I felt like a teenager again, though back then I didn't have a cell phone. My mother wouldn't let me. She said land line phones were completely acceptable. I was embarrassed because all my friends had them.

"Oh." Connor pulled out a chair and flopped into it. He still had on shorts and a wrinkly T-shirt from bed. His little legs swung back and forth, as his feet didn't yet touch the ground. "Can I go swimming today?"

I sat down with my mug of coffee after handing him a glass of chocolate milk. "*May* I ... and of course! It's already hot out. I thought we could take a cooler with some drinks and sandwiches and just spend the day at our beach."

"Awesome!" That perked him up.

He sure did love water. I was happy he liked the water, but afraid as well. I didn't want to live in constant fear because of what happened to my brother but couldn't seem to turn it off. I definitely didn't want to transmit that fear to my kids, though they already knew I was Nervous Nellie when it came to them being in the water.

"Can I ... *may* I have some cereal, please?" Connor asked.

"Of course you *may*."

I stood up and grabbed cereal and milk and a bowl for Connor and then started making sandwiches for our picnic. It would be a little while until we headed to our beach, but I wanted to be prepared.

After breakfast, Connor and I headed to our rooms to get ready. As I pulled on my bathing suit and began to pack a beach bag, my thoughts roamed to James. I hadn't heard from him in a few days and that made me sad. I cared for him—loved him, even—but I didn't see how I could just jump back into a relationship with him. Didn't we have a lot to talk about? I had been sixteen the last time we were together. That's a long time. Maybe I was making more of it than I should have. And honestly, I think I was more scared than "not ready." With Greg it was ... safe. I wasn't "in love" with him and he knew it, but he took care of us and protected us, and he gave me Connor. Was I really ready to start fresh with James? Or pick up where we left off?

I did a quick check of my phone again. Nothing. I heaved a sigh. I supposed I could text him, but ... what would I say?

Shake it off, Ell. Deep breath.

"Ok, sweetie, I'm ready!" I called out to Connor as I set the cooler and beach bag by the door.

Connor came running down the stairs, beach towel in hand and a big grin on his face. He helped me carry some things, and we headed towards the water.

After we settled our stuff and spread the blanket out, Connor ran right into the water, shrieking at the initial cold shock, and I sat in the beach chair. I wanted to keep a close eye on Connor, but I also wanted to do some reading. I pulled my mother's journal out from my beach bag. It wasn't the best for beach reading, but it had to be done.

After giving Connor a wave and a smile, I opened the journal to where I left off. The next entry I read disturbed me a bit, as my mother mentioned my grandmother's possible memory loss and … dementia? I shook my head. I didn't think Grandma had dementia back then, though I did recall a few times she had forgotten certain things or couldn't find something she had lost. But that was normal … right? I think back then I was in denial about my grandma getting older. We had been much closer than my mother and I, so I hadn't wanted my grandma to get older.

I did remember a few times she forgot meals or where we had been if we went to the beach. Did I remember her forgetting Johnny at any point? I didn't think so.

I shook my head and continued reading.

July 5

Yesterday was amazing. Mother and I took the kids to town for the annual barbecue and fireworks. Johnny loved watching them. He loves fireworks. Ellie was distracted, probably looking for James. They usually spent the Fourth together, but this time they didn't for some reason. When fireworks were finished, Mom took the kids back to the house after I insisted I had promised the other ladies in town I'd help clean up. That was a bunch of posh. I was meeting Sam.

I didn't get home til almost two in the morning. We had the most amazing night.

I stopped reading, feeling sick to my stomach. So my mother *was* sneaking around. My father had been dead for three years at that time, but why did Mom have to hide Sam from us?

I watched my son splash around the water, pretending he was some sort of fish. He sure acted like a fish. I laughed at some of his antics and then drummed up the nerve to continue reading.

Sam makes me feel whole. Even before Ben died, Sam just had a way of making me feel more loved than my own husband. I look at Johnny and feel sad that he can't have a relationship with his father, but it just isn't to be.

There it was again—the mention of Johnny's father. I still hadn't figured out if she meant my dad or Sam. I didn't want to skip ahead in the journal entries because I wanted to make sure I didn't miss anything, so I'd have to wait to find out. I kept reading the July fifth passage but skimmed through the rest as it was very detailed from their night together.

Once I finished with that entry, I closed the journal and stuffed it into my bag. I had enough for a bit. I sat there stewing. I needed to go to town. I wanted answers. Gert would know who Sam Davis was, and I was determined to meet him. How did I not know this man? If we were here every summer, how would I not have met him? I was so angry at my mother for this mess!!

My dilemma was figuring out how to meet Sam without taking Connor with me. It was too bad I hadn't spoken to James in a few days; he'd do something fun with Connor so I could sneak into town. *Oh my goodness; I sounded like my mother! Sneak into town?? Good grief.*

Later that evening, Connor and I ate hot dogs and

chips—Connor's favorite meal—then he ran outside to play with his trucks while I finished cleaning up the kitchen. I knew Morgan would be home shortly, but I didn't want to leave her with Connor to run to town. Not this late in the evening. I could call Gert but would rather talk face-to-face.

"Mommy, Morgan is home!" I heard my son yell from outside. I quickly wiped the counter and set the towel down.

"Hey, slimeball," Morgan said to her brother.

"*You're* a slimeball!" was Connor's retort. They both laughed.

I shook my head and walked outside. Morgan looked tired but she was smiling. She set her backpack down and was crouched down, looking at what her brother was doing. He had built a "garage" for his trucks using big stones he found by the water. A part of me was angry for him going to the water alone, but he looked so happy talking to his sister, I just couldn't break his heart. I'd have to talk to him later about it, though.

"Hi, honey. Did you have fun today?"

"Yeah. We hiked a long way, but it was cool. I took pics on my phone." Morgan grabbed her bag and walked over to me. "I saw James in town when me and my friends grabbed some ice cream."

"Oh, yeah?" I answered casually, trying not to let any emotions show on my face.

"Yeah. He asked about you. Are you two not talking?" Her eyes were narrowed.

"It's ... complicated."

Morgan rolled her eyes. "That's what adults say when they don't want to answer. I'm going to shower."

I watched Morgan walk inside. She had been right; I didn't want to answer. I really didn't know what the answer was.

"Mommy, can we make a fire tonight and have s'mores?" Connor asked, breaking my thoughts.

I had a strong desire to decline. I wanted to be alone so

I could read more of the journal, but I needed to spend time with my kids first. I'd make time for the journal later.

Smiling at Connor, I said, "Sure, honey. Let's wait for Morgan."

"Yay!!" Connor jumped up and ran inside, no doubt hunting for ingredients to make s'mores.

The journal would have to wait.

* * * * *

"I want another one!"

"Hold *on*, Connor!"

"Ok, kids, that's enough," I finally spoke, tired of listening to them argue. They both had their fair share of s'mores and then began arguing about who would get the next turn. It was after nine, and I could tell Connor was overtired, but the kids were having fun and I didn't want to ruin it for them.

Morgan pulled out a marshmallow and threw the bag at Connor. He grinned and grabbed *two* marshmallows then stuck his tongue out at his sister. I shook my head.

Our fire pit was blazing brilliantly, and the moon in the sky reflected off the water. It was a chilly night, and I was glad I made everyone dress in jeans and long-sleeve shirts.

"Ok, guys, last one, then it's time to wind down," I told the kids. Connor groaned but I knew he'd pass right out once his head hit the pillow. We had a great evening telling "ghost" stories and discussing the upcoming school year and the fun things we had already done over the summer. I would cherish memories of that time with my kids.

The kids ate the last of their treat and we began picking up to head up to the house. I was just grabbing the trash bag, when I heard footsteps.

"I guess I missed the party."

I froze. I looked up and saw James standing near us wearing jeans and a long-sleeved shirt. He had a timid smile on his face, almost as if he wasn't sure if he should be there.

"I invited him, Mom," Morgan admitted somewhat

sheepishly.

"Oh, I'm sorry, James. We were just picking up," I told him.

"*Mo-ommmm,*" Morgan huffed in frustration. "I told him to come at nine because then you two could be alone. Seems you two have to talk."

Good Lord, when did my daughter become so grown up? I sighed, knowing she was right. I put on a smile, and we began walking towards the house, Connor chatting excitedly, telling James how many s'mores he ate "without puking."

"Gross," Morgan muttered.

"Ok, kids, go wash up. Connor, I'll be up soon to tuck you in."

"Ok, Mom!"

Morgan said a quick "goodnight" and hurried into the house. James and I followed, then went into the kitchen to put things away. We did this in silence, knowing our talk would come soon enough.

"Ready, Mommy!" Connor shouted from upstairs.

"I'll be right back," I told James. "Help yourself to anything."

James nodded, and I walked out of the kitchen, my heart racing in anticipation of what our conversation would entail. I climbed the steps to the loft, hoping our goodnights would be quick.

"Ok, kiddo, you ready to … Connor?" I entered my son's room to find him standing by the window, staring outside. The kids both had a window that looked over the yard and the lake.

"Honey?"

"Mommy, will the little boy get hurt by the fire?"

"*What??*" Chills coursed through my body as I felt my heart skip a beat. "What little boy?"

"That one. He's standing by the fire we had." Connor pointed at the window, and I hurried over. I looked through the glass and saw our fire pit, the flames still blazing, but I didn't see anyone there.

"Honey, there is no one out there." I pulled his arm gently to pry him away from the window. His eyes were wide and his face paper white as he turned to face me. "Connor, baby, it's just tricks by the flames, ok?" *This kid is scaring me!*

He nodded slowly, and with one last glance out the window, he crawled into bed. I tucked him in and gave him a kiss. He was quiet, but his eyes were drooping. He was probably just imagining things, being as tired as he was.

"Sweet dreams," I whispered, then clicked his lamp off and walked over to Morgan's room. She was in bed actually holding a book! Finally, she was doing some summer reading. I wondered if James had anything to do with that. "Night, sweetie."

Morgan looked up and smiled. "Night, Mom." Then she winked. *Oh, gosh.* I just rolled my eyes.

I headed downstairs to resume my night and found James waiting in the kitchen holding a beer in one hand and a glass of wine in the other. He handed me the wine as if it were a peace offering. I smiled and took the glass.

"James, Connor said something disturbing."

"Oh yeah?"

I nodded as we walked towards the back porch. The door creaked, reminding me that there were still a few more things I needed to take care of around the house. "He asked if the little boy would be ok by the fire."

James looked at me quizzically. "Little boy?"

"Mm hmm. I didn't see anyone, but it freaked me out. He has mentioned this little boy before."

We walked back to the fire pit. I didn't see anyone around, and didn't expect to, but Connor's words chilled me.

"Ell, does he know about your brother? Did you ever tell the kids?"

"No, not Connor. Morgan knows because she found some pictures once and asked, but I didn't want to tell

Connor." I sat on the ground near the fire pit and James sat next to me. The chairs had already been taken up, but I didn't mind sitting on the grass. I brought my knees up to my chest, wrapping one arm around them.

"He's old enough to be told, Ell. He should know about his uncle."

"His *dead* uncle, you mean." I laughed, even though it wasn't funny. I took a sip of wine and became serious. "This place is … it's weird."

"Strange things have been happening, Ellie, but they can probably be explained."

I rolled my eyes. Why was James so logical? Would it be so bad if Johnny and Grandma remained here in spirit? They weren't hurting anything. Not really.

James and I watched the flames dance. A slight breeze kicked up, and I shivered a little and edged closer to the fire.

"So, Morgan called you? I didn't realize you had exchanged numbers," I said lightly.

"She's my daughter, Ellie. I am going to keep in touch with her."

I nodded, not looking over at him. "I know," I whispered.

James inched closer to me, and my hands began to tremble. James has been the only man to ever make me feel like I was in love all over again.

"Morgan wanted you and I to talk. I think teenagers have this weird intuition," James said.

I gave a little laugh. "They sure do. Try figuring out a teenager someday. Can't do it." I took another sip of wine, feeling relaxed. The night was so peaceful and the setting romantic. *Oh gee. Do I want romantic?*

"Look, I want a relationship with Morgan, and I've grown very fond of Connor. And you know how I feel about you."

"Ok … " I turned to look at James, his eyes fierce with determination. With the flames from the fire reflecting in his eyes, they were quite intense. He had already told me this before. Why was he bringing it up again?

"If it's ok with you, I want to move closer to you guys. My work can be done anywhere. I can see the kids and get to know Morgan, and maybe … ." James didn't finish the sentence, but I knew what he was going to say.

"Maybe we can see where this is headed?" I finished.

"Yes," James whispered. He was leaning closer to me, and I could feel the sparks fly—not from the flames but between us. Then he kissed me softly, and I let myself fall into the kiss because I wanted it just as much as he did. The connection I felt with James all those years ago was still there. As our kiss deepened, my heart soared at the love I had for him.

Eventually, James pulled back and looked deep into my eyes. "I think we're going to be just fine, Miss Elise."

We sat a little longer, not saying a word—no words were needed—watching the dark lake water and listening to the night sounds. How different it was from home. I still didn't want to keep the lake house. Maybe someday I could get another lake house. Somewhere else.

Finally, we doused the flames and headed back to the house. I felt such peace; I didn't want the feeling to end. James took my hand as we walked towards the house, and I looked up—out of habit—and stopped dead in my tracks.

"What's wrong?" James asked, looking at me.

"The window. There's … there's a boy in the window." I pointed to Connor's bedroom window, and James looked up.

"There isn't anyone there, Ell."

"He was just there!! Not Connor. Someone else!" I shouted and took off running. I ran into the house and flew up the stairs and into Connor's room.

Connor was sound asleep in his bed, and there was no one else there with him.

Chapter 21

It took days for me to recover from the person I saw—or *thought* I saw—in Connor's window. James had looked around the house and outside as well but didn't see anyone, and I don't think he expected to.

It didn't make sense. I had to let it go, though. I had to stop thinking about my brother and spirits or ghosts or whatever the hell was in that house.

On a warm Saturday, I drove the kids into town for the annual craft fair which was held the last week in July, and it was amazing. Vendors from all over the county set up tents selling baked goods, books, apparel, jewelry, soaps, and a variety of other handmade items.

I always loved the craft fair as a child and was happy to see they continued the tradition years later. It was one good memory I had of spending summers at the lake. Grandma would give me and Johnny a little spending money, and we'd have fun picking out knick knacks and fudge and whatever else we could find that was "cool" or super sugary! I had done the same with my kids—given them spending money—as I wanted them to share in the experiences I had at their ages.

"You know," Morgan said as we drove into town. "I

could get used to this place. I wouldn't mind coming again next summer."

I laughed, partly because I was surprised and partly because there was no way I'd be coming back to the lake house. It held too many damned secrets, too many memories and a lot of heartache. The only good thing that had come from any of it was my daughter. Well ... and James.

"I was thinking next year for vacation we'd check out a bigger resort town and stay in a hotel that had a pool and other fun things," was my response.

"Yay!" Connor shouted from the back seat.

I found a parking spot close to the park, and after turning off the engine, I turned to my kids. "We're going to walk around for a bit then meet James for lunch, ok? Stay close together and don't stray too far from me."

The kids nodded and unbuckled their belts, hurrying out of the car. It was a perfect day—not too hot, just warm enough—and the town was bustling with locals and tourists.

We walked around the park for over an hour, checking out every tent full of goodies. There were so many vendors! I loved the homemade items, while Morgan was drawn to the artsy tables—paintings, dreamcatchers, caricature drawings—and Connor stayed close to a man who carved cars and trucks out of wood and painted them. I'd have to keep that in mind and grab one for him for his next birthday before we left.

I was looking at a pretty floral kitchen towel set, thinking it would go well in my kitchen at home, when someone bumped into me. I looked up as the person said, "Excuse me; sorry!"

I gasped. The man touched my arm and looked concerned. "I'm sorry, ma'am, are you hurt?"

I shook my head but couldn't stop staring. It was him—the man who bumped into me was Sam Davis.

I couldn't speak. I was finally face-to-face with the

mysterious Sam Davis and I couldn't speak!

"Ok … well, have a good day," Sam mumbled with a quizzical glance and turned to walk away.

"Wait!" I shouted.

With a puzzled expression on his face, Sam turned around. I had no idea what to say then. *Hey, did you sleep with my mother? By the way, my brother may be your child.* Ugh, how would I go about approaching the subject to get answers?

I don't know how long I stood there looking like an idiot, but I finally gathered my wits. I quickly glanced over my shoulder to make sure my kids were not in earshot—they were busy looking at fudge two tables away—and I turned back to Sam.

"Did you know my mother? June. June Roberts," I blurted out. *Ok, that was a little dumb.*

Sam's confused expression quickly changed to surprise. His eyes flickered around the park then back to me. He moved closer and, in almost a whisper, asked, "Who wants to know?"

I pulled back in surprise. "I do. I'm her daughter."

"Not here. Please."

"Ok, well, where? And when? I'm at my family's lake house for the summer and I've discovered some … disturbing things."

"Fine, fine. Give me an hour, then meet me over at Landsey's Edge. You know the place?"

"I do. I'll see you then."

Sam walked away without another word, and I stood there, wondering what I had gotten myself into.

"Mommy, can we get fudge?"

I turned to see Connor and Morgan holding boxes of fudge, so I walked over to pay, not remembering that they had their own spending money. If I wasn't in shock over finally meeting Sam, I would have chuckled at their slyness.

"Can't have any until after lunch," I told the kids, handing them their bags of fudge. *Crap. We are supposed to meet James for lunch.* I really wanted to meet Sam. I hoped I could talk James into having lunch with the kids alone so I could go. Apparently, I hadn't thought it out before I agreed to Sam's time.

We walked around a bit longer and then made our way to the café where James was waiting. He had a grin on his face when he saw us and looked especially handsome in his tan shorts, button-down blue shirt that made his eyes practically glow, and his tanned body. I shook my thoughts away. Couldn't be thinking about his body at that moment.

"Hey," I greeted. "I need to talk to you for a sec." I pulled him away from the café so the kids wouldn't hear, then I explained my dilemma.

"Are you sure you want to meet with him alone?" James asked, looking concerned.

I had to laugh. "James, it's a busy place and he won't try to hurt me. Besides, according to you he's well-known around here." *Hence the reason he wanted to meet alone, no doubt.*

"No, Ell … I mean, you may hear things you don't want to hear or aren't *ready* to hear. Maybe Gert can keep an eye on the kids, and I can go with you."

I shook my head. "No, James. This is *my* deal. Just tell the kids I had to run an errand and we'll meet back at the house. Please?"

James looked at me for a second then sighed. "Ok but call me the minute you need me."

"I will. Always the protector, aren't you?" I gave him a playful shove then quickly said goodbye to the kids and walked back to my car. Finally, I was going to get answers.

I drove a few miles to the restaurant and, after parking, sat in the car for a minute. I had to drum up the nerve to talk to Sam. This was my time to get answers to questions I couldn't ask my mother. I had to do this.

With a deep breath, I climbed out of the car and walked towards the building. Landsey's Edge was a small restaurant by the water. It wasn't anything fancy, but it was clean, and the locals loved it. They *did* have the best fish fry around; I had been there once or twice in my lifetime.

I walked in and spotted Sam sitting at a table near the window in the corner away from most patrons. He was already sipping on a beer.

"Thanks for meeting me," I said as I slid into the seat across from him. The waitress hurried over and I ordered a water.

Sam took a swig of his beer and nodded. He wasn't an unattractive man. His hair was gray, his eyes were brown, and he had a gentle face. He had a good build for his age. I figured he kept fit by the farm work. "So, what would you like to know?"

I took a deep breath. "I don't know if you remembered what happened to my family years ago," I started.

"Sure. June's boy drowned, didn't he?"

Ok, that was blunt. "Yes, it was tragic. She never recovered." I ignored Sam's raised eyebrows and continued. "Did you know her and my grandma well?"

"Sure—I mean, I've been in this town all my life, and your family came up to the lake house every summer. I knew your granddad too; we were friends." Sam finished his beer and held his glass to the waitress as she set my water down. *This is like pulling teeth.*

"Get ya'll anything?" the waitress asked. She was cute—probably early fifties—and it was clear Sam was checking her out. Was he some sort of playboy? I didn't even know if he was married! I saw him with someone the day we ran into each other for the first time. Was that just a girlfriend?

"I'll have the fish platter," Sam told her.

"Um, same, please." I wasn't terribly hungry—my stomach was in knots, actually—but I ordered to keep the conversation going. When the waitress walked away, I turned back to Sam. "Look, I'm going to just say it." Sam waited, his eyebrows raised. "Did you and my mom … I mean, did you—"

"Honey, look," Sam interrupted. "I knew your mom well, ok? I also was good friends with your grandparents. We all knew each other around here. Whatever happened to your mom, anyway? I never saw her after ... well, you know."

I sat, unsure of what to say next as Sam gulped down his beer. How did he not have a beer belly? Maybe he didn't drink that much. I suddenly noticed him staring at me. "Ok, you knew my family ... fine. I probably even met you when I was a kid. But what I am asking is—"

Sam laughed, interrupting me yet again. The man was beginning to become infuriating. "Elise, I never met you in my life. Sure, I saw you around town when your mom brought you up here for the summer, but she never introduced her kids to us."

"You knew about Johnny?"

Sam shrugged. "Ok, her boy was named Johnny. Now I know. Look, I'm not a heartless man, I just don't know why we're here and why you're asking these questions."

Before I could respond, the waitress brought over our fish platters. Our plates were piled high with breaded haddock, baby shrimp, French fries and coleslaw. The food looked and smelled delicious, but whatever appetite I once had left with Sam's aloof attitude.

The waitress walked away, after winking at Sam, and Sam dug in. I took a bite of my fish—it *was* heavenly—and chewed thoughtfully. Sam was blunt, for sure, but I had to be careful not to get him on the defense. Clearly, he had never met Johnny. Did he know he had a son?

We ate in silence for a few minutes, and I waved the waitress over to order a glass of white wine. I hadn't been planning on drinking, but my nerves were on edge, and I needed to calm down. When the drink was set in front of me, I took a long sip of the cool liquid and then sat back.

"You want to know what happened to my mom? My mom had a nervous breakdown after her son drowned, and she never recovered. To this day, she sits almost unresponsive in a mental institution. My grandmother died in her lake house all alone. I'm just now finding family secrets! I want answers." Taking a deep breath, I drank more of my wine, satisfied that I had blurted everything out.

Sam nodded slowly. "I'm sorry to hear about your brother," he said softly. "A child's death is … well, it's a horrible thing."

"It was. I'll never forget that day."

"You were young, weren't you?" Sam asked.

I nodded, taking another sip of wine. Sam had finished eating and was sitting back, sipping his beer now instead of guzzling it. He was steering clear of the other issues I mentioned, but that was ok with me.

"I was sixteen. Look, Sam, I just want to know if you and my mom … well, you know."

"What? *Seeing* each other? Naw, just friends." His eyes shifted slightly when he responded.

I narrowed my eyes. This was going to be more difficult than I thought. Sam and Johnny resembled each other—that was no coincidence. "My mother used to sneak into town, and she wrote things about you and her in her journal. So, you can either tell me the truth, or I'll dig around until I find it out myself," I challenged.

"Ok, ok," Sam held his hands up in surrender. "Look, I liked your mother … a lot. We had a good time when she came up each summer. Is that so wrong? She was a widow!"

"She wasn't a widow at first! You two were having an affair before that; I know it!" I hissed, trying not to raise my voice and gain attention from the other diners. I peeked around and noticed the dining area was filling up. I had to be quieter. "If my mother hadn't been in town with *you* that day, Johnny never would have died!"

Sam sat there in stunned silence. "Ok, kid. Look, I'm sorry. But why bring this up now? And why bring it up to *me?*"

"Because my brother resembles you so much, I think you're his father," I finished. I glanced at my wine glance, noticing it was empty.

I noticed Sam was sweating and his hands were shaking. He pulled out his wallet and threw a few twenty-dollar bills down and stood up. "Not possible. June would have told me if I had a son."

I stood up as well, grabbing my purse. "Sam, look. I just want to find answers."

"If I were you, I'd let it all remain buried. Even if that kid were mine, he's not here anymore, so there's no point in going back to the past." And with that, Sam walked out of the restaurant, leaving me in stunned silence.

I flagged the waitress down for one more glass of wine, not caring about the food anymore, and sat there, staring into space. This definitely had not gone as planned.

Later, when I returned to the house, I had to put on a happy face for the kids. They were playing catch in the yard with James, and everyone looked so happy. Like a family.

"Hi, Mommy!" Connor shouted from the yard.

I gave him a wave and a grin, then walked inside to change. I had been wearing nice shorts and a blouse with my sandals, but now I just wanted my running pants and a T-shirt. Comfort is what I needed.

When I came back outside, James was waiting for me on the porch, and I told him about the conversation with Sam and how I felt. His response wasn't what I wanted to hear.

"Ellie, what did you expect? Did you think it would have a happy ending like the Disney movies? This is real life. Sam is stunned."

I shook my head and walked towards the lake. "Why would he walk away?" I asked James, crossing my arms. "I told him he may have a son, and he walked away!"

"Ell," James said softly. "He *had* a son. Remember that. Even if Sam believes Johnny was his son, Johnny isn't here. How do you imagine Sam would be feeling?"

I didn't respond. Instead, I watched my kids play for a few minutes. They were so happy and carefree. Why couldn't I be like that? Why did I insist on dredging up the past? Though, lately, it felt like the past was dredging itself up.

It was just about evening, and the air was getting cooler. I began to shiver. James stepped up behind me and wrapped his arms around me. His touch was a comfort. I didn't know if I wanted to cry; I didn't know if I had tears left.

"I just want a connection to Johnny," I said softly.

"I know you do. I know." He nuzzled his face in my neck, and it felt so good … so right.

We stood there for a few minutes until Connor ran over. "Mom, did you see that catch? I'm getting—hey, Mom, are you ok?"

I pulled away from James and looked at my son, who was visibly concerned. "I'm fine, sweetie. Sometimes I get sad. James was just giving me a hug."

"I'll give you a hug anytime!" Connor exclaimed. "But did you see that catch?" He ran off back to his sister without a care in the world.

I took a deep breath. "Thanks, James. You know, for being here for me."

"I'm here as long as you need me," James whispered.

I nodded. "I'm going to make some supper. Do you want to stay?" I had to get busy with something.

"I better not. I promised Gert I'd make a delivery for her, and then I need to get to bed early. I'm helping Charlie bright and early."

"Ok." I understood. James often helped his friend Charlie with his horses. I remembered my mom taking Johnny and I to Charlie's stables a few times when we were at the lake house. Johnny loved riding. Maybe Connor would like to try this summer. Charlie had to be ancient by now, but he was so kind and much-loved in the community.

"Hey, guys, I'm heading out!" James called to the kids.

They both came running over, and Connor reached his arms out for a hug. My heart melted seeing James kneel and take my son into his arms. Morgan stood there shyly but had a smile on her face.

"Bye, James. Thanks for lunch," Morgan said.

"Ok, kids, let's go get some grub."

"*Mo-om,*" Morgan groaned. "No one calls it 'grub.'"

Connor laughed. "Gross grub!"

We all laughed and made our way up to the house. James waved and walked to his truck as the kids and I went inside to get some "grub."

Chapter 22

My mother's journal sat in my lap as I pushed the porch swing back and forth with my feet. The moon shone brightly on the still lake water. Somewhere in the dark, an owl hooted, insects chirped, and the occasional frog could be heard. When I was younger, I don't think I ever appreciated nature. Now, as an adult … well, I could get used to living like this (obviously not at *this* particular place, though). The hustle and bustle of the city breaks you down after a while unless you're the type of person who can handle the constant on-the-go and rush-rush of city life. I wasn't that person but had conformed to it.

I was exhausted from the day. My conversation with Sam had me on edge. I really hadn't gotten anywhere with him. Maybe it was just best to let it all lie.

"Mom!"

Ugh. It was after eight and I thought the kids were settled for the night. I know Morgan doesn't go to bed that early, but she was listening to her iPod when I came outside. Now Connor was calling me for some reason.

With a sigh, I walked into the house and up to my son's room. He was sitting on the bed, holding his favorite teddy.

"What's wrong?" I asked. I looked around the small

area but didn't see anything out of the ordinary.

"I saw him again," Connor said, his voice shaking.

"Saw who?"

"*Him*," Connor whispered.

"Connor, there is no one up here, and ghosts don't exist!" Morgan shouted from the other room.

"I did too see someone!" Connor shouted back.

"Ok, ok," I said, trying to keep my cool. I wasn't in the mood for this right now. "Where did you see someone?"

Connor pointed to the window, and my veins turned to ice. I walked over and looked out but didn't see anyone outside—thank God, because I had just been sitting there. I turned back to my son and sat on the bed.

"Connor, your imagination is in overdrive. There's no one out there, ok?"

"But—"

"But nothing!" I took a deep breath, trying not to show my anger. I was tired of him saying he saw a little boy. I shuddered at the thought that it could be Johnny's spirit roaming around. But Connor didn't know about Johnny, so …

"Try to get some sleep," I told him.

"Ok, Mommy." Connor enveloped me in a big hug, and I heard him whisper, *"It will be ok, sissy."*

I jumped back, startling Connor. "What did you just say?"

Connor shook his head and tears pooled in his eyes. "I didn't say anything, Mommy," he said, his voice shaking.

"Connor Gregory, tell me the truth *right now!*" I shouted.

"Mom, what's going on?"

I whipped around to see Morgan standing in the doorway. "Did you tell your brother about Johnny?" I asked, almost in a whisper. I felt tears brimming in my eyes, and I was shaking.

Morgan shook her head; her eyes were wide with concern.

"Who is Johnny?" Connor asked.

"No one." *Deep breath, in and out.* "I'm sorry, sweetie. Mommy is tired. I need to … I need to go lie down."

I walked downstairs as if in a trance, then I strolled into the living room and stood in front of the window, staring out into the darkness.

What had Connor seen? Could Johnny's spirit really be here? Was he really telling me it would be ok?

"I'm losing it," I mumbled. I turned the lights off, got ready for bed, and tossed and turned until after four in the morning. I kept hearing Connor—Johnny?—whispering to me: *"It will be ok, sissy."*

* * * * *

Howling wind woke me up and I sat up quickly. I was disoriented for a minute until I realized I was in bed, and a quick glance at my clock told me it was barely five in the morning. I stood up and went to the window. The sky was dark, and the wind was so fierce the tree branches were practically dancing. *Great,* I thought. *We'll probably lose power.* I was wide awake, so I decided to brew some coffee in case we did lose power. I had the percolator just in case, but still … the coffee maker was easier.

When I walked into the kitchen, I spotted my mother's journal on the table. Where had that come from? I didn't remember bringing it in from the night before or even putting it on the table. Odd. I shrugged and started the coffee maker. It wasn't set to brew for a while, but I needed it now.

While the coffee was brewing, I went back to my room to throw on shorts and a sweatshirt. I'm not sure why I even bothered getting dressed; it seemed like we'd be inside all day with the pending storm.

Finally, the coffee was ready, so I filled a mug and headed to the back porch. The wind was so fierce, the porch swing was swaying back and forth by itself, and my hair whipped around my face. Feeling annoyed, I hurried back inside to get a clip to pull my hair up away from my face. Morgan didn't think it was cool that I still wore my hair past my shoulders, but I didn't care; I loved my long hair. Who said women in their thirties couldn't have long hair??

Hair up and coffee mug back in hand, I once again stepped outside, this time pulling the door shut behind me before it could slam on my rear.

I walked down to the water's edge and stood there, watching the raging waves crash against the rocks. I didn't see birds or geese, and there were no calming sounds of the morning, just fierce wind. I felt a few rain drops, but I didn't care. I stood there staring at the lake—the very lake that took my brother's life sixteen years ago.

Johnny would be twenty-one now. He'd be in college, probably, and hanging out with friends. Maybe he'd have a girlfriend. I wondered what he would look like at that age. He had been a cute kid; no doubt he would have been a handsome adult. Sometimes I thought I saw a little of Johnny in Connor's facial expressions.

I'm not sure how long I stood there; time seemed to slip away. As the rain became more intense, I turned to hurry back to the house. Suddenly, I spotted something in the water down by the beach. I squinted my eyes but couldn't make out the shape. It couldn't be a person—there wasn't anyone nearby except James, and he wouldn't be in the water. No, it was small, almost like a child ... or animal?

I stood there frozen, rain pounding on my body and wind whipping at my face. *What ... who ...* I couldn't move.

"Mom?" Morgan was yelling from somewhere close by.

I stood there staring. I had to move; I had to do something! I wasn't able to save my brother sixteen years ago, so if it was within my power to save someone now, I was going to do it!

I dropped my mug and was about to run to the beach, when someone grabbed my arm, and I screamed.

"Mom! It's me!" Morgan was holding my arm, looking

very concerned.

"Morgan, let go! I need to—we need to save that … " I looked over to the beach and saw nothing in the water.

"Mom?" Morgan's voice was barely heard through the wind and rain, but she sounded frightened.

"I saw someone. I know I did!" *Didn't I?*

"Come on inside, Mom. You're scaring me."

I followed Morgan inside with one last look at the beach.

It was empty.

Morgan reached for my hand and gently pulled me into the house. She prodded me to change my clothes and then lie on the couch while she made me decaf, saying I definitely did not need caffeine.

I curled up under a blanket on the couch, listening to the rain beat on the windows. My head was pounding. I know what I saw; I know there was someone in that water. What if they were still there? What if they drowned?

My heart was beating anxiously, but I was so tired. The room was so cozy with the small lamp lit and Morgan's scented candle burning nearby. The sound of rain outside.

My eyes were slowly closing when I heard the front door open and click shut. I sat up with a jolt and listened. No one made a sound, yet I heard rustling as if someone was pulling off their coat. Silence. Then footsteps. I waited.

"Ellie?"

I turned my head slowly. "James," I whispered and sat up. My eyes welled up with tears, and he rushed over to me. He sat next to me and hugged me tightly.

"Are you ok?" he asked softly, rubbing my back. "Morgan called, and—"

"I'm ok," I sniffed. "I saw... I thought … "

James pulled back and looked into my eyes, looking terribly worried. "Ell—"

"James," I stopped him before he continued. "I know what you're going to say."

"What, Ellie? You know I'm going to tell you that you

need to let Johnny go?"

I pulled back quickly. "What? No! I mean … *what?*"

"Honey, we all faced a horrible tragedy all of those years ago, but you have to let Johnny be at rest! You found your mother's journal, you discovered secrets, you found your brother's belongings. You haven't rested since you've been here!"

"Have so," I muttered, feeling childish. I stood up and began pacing. Where were the kids? It was quiet. My arms were crossed over my chest as I turned to face James. "Look, I found secrets my family had been keeping from me. Is it so wrong to finish uncovering them?"

"Not if," James began as he stood up and crossed the room, standing in front of me, "it means you begin seeing things and becoming … well, crazy."

James knew I hated that word. My mother was crazy; I was not. Sure, I had gone through therapy sessions as a teenager. I mean, who wouldn't? I was a pregnant teenager who lost her brother and mother in one summer! But I wasn't *crazy*.

When Morgan was just six months old, I had gone through an awful depression and started drinking a lot. My aunt—bless her heart—took over caring for my baby while I saw a therapist and went to rehab. Therapy helped, but returning to the lake house was undoing everything I had gotten through all those years ago. I wasn't sure I could ever let go now.

"Why does Connor keep seeing someone?" I challenged, willing the conversation to continue.

"Do you really think your brother's spirit is here? Why wouldn't he be at rest, Elise?"

Elise? Oof, this was getting serious. "I don't know. Maybe … " I had nothing. James was right. Why *would* Johnny return? He'd be in Heaven for sure. Wouldn't he?

I returned to the couch and flopped down. *Was* I going crazy? Well, if *I* was going crazy, then Connor was too. He was seeing things. I shook the thought out of my head. I needed to sleep.

As if James could read my thoughts, he walked over and pulled the blanket back over my body. "Rest, Ellie. We'll talk tomorrow." After a kiss on my forehead, he walked out of the room.

I laid down and let sleep take over, not caring if I slept all day. I didn't know if James had left or not, but I knew sleep was dragging me under, and I was ok with that.

Chapter 23

The next couple of weeks were uneventful. I had calmed down from everything that had happened so far, and I even forgot—almost—that my grandmother's body was buried on our property. It helped that I kept busy so my mind wouldn't wander too much.

When Morgan wasn't working at the store, we hung out at the beach or took hikes in our woods or on one of the nearby mountain trails. When she was working, Connor kept busy either swimming or playing with toys and even helped me around the house a bit. I was still trying to update the house a little and fix it up to make it appealing to potential buyers without taking away its personality. Of course, there was the matter of a dead body on the property. I needed to have her removed before I could sell the house. I didn't want to leave my grandma behind when strangers moved in.

The days passed without any mention of a "little boy outside" or me seeing someone in the water, so I counted that as a plus. I somehow managed to push everything that had happened so far out of my thoughts so I could concentrate on spending time with the kids and getting the house ready for sale.

August came around, and I was finally satisfied with the progress on the house. Painting was finished, loose boards were nailed down, the basement was emptied, and overall, the house was definitely sellable. I had mixed feelings about it now that past secrets were coming to light, and I was trying to deal with them. I definitely didn't want to keep the house, but I would miss it in a way. I had great memories growing up there, especially as a teenager.

James and I were growing closer. It felt like old times when we would spend nearly every day together. He often stopped by to visit or have supper with me and the kids. I was even pleased that he took Morgan to dinner after she was done with her shift at the store one evening. They wanted to get to know each other more, and I had resigned myself to the fact that he was in her life now to stay. I was ok with that; I just didn't know where James and I stood. I had fallen in love all over again when I first saw him after I arrived at the beginning of summer, but what would happen after we left in a few weeks?

"Mommy, can I go fishing with James?"

I had been washing dishes and lost in thought when Connor came into the kitchen. He was still in his sleep wear but had been playing with his trucks on the back porch—after promising not to leave the porch without telling me, of course.

"*May* I. And is James here?" I asked, wiping my hands dry.

"Hey, Ellie. I'm heading out to do some fishing, and I thought Connor may want to go along." James was standing in the doorway wearing cut-off jean shorts and a T-shirt. I shook my head and laughed.

"James, tell me those are *not* the same jean shorts you wore when you were a teenager!" I exclaimed in mock horror. He had been obsessed with those shorts for two summers straight. I used to tease him endlessly … though his rear end *did* look good in them.

James only grinned. "Nah, I don't fit into those

anymore. Made myself some new ones."

I rolled my eyes good-naturedly. "Good Lord. Ok, Connor, you may go with James—"

"Yay!" Connor shouted.

"BUT! You need to get dressed first. And make sure your teeth are brushed!" I yelled to him as he ran out of the room. Turning to James, I said, "Thanks for taking him. I think I'll take some time to finish reading Mom's journal entries."

"Ell, I think you need to let it lie. Burn the damn journal. Sam obviously didn't know about Johnny—if he *is* his father—and clearly doesn't care now to know. Let it go, hon."

"I can't, James. You know I can't. I *need* to find out the truth. You know about your daughter now. Don't you think Sam has the right to know about Johnny whether he wants to or not?"

James only shook his head. "Ok, Ell, but you've been a bit unsteady lately with your emotions. Remember the lake incident."

"You don't have to remind me about that," I snapped. I took a deep breath. "Look, I know you mean well, but it's something I need to do. We're leaving in a few weeks, the house will be sold, and I just want to uncover the secrets so I can get past them."

"Will you?"

"What?"

"Get past them. Will you?" James stepped closer to me and placed his hands on my waist. I set my hands on his firm upper arms and gazed into his eyes. My hands trailed up to his neck as he leaned in, gently kissing me.

Connor chose that moment to run into the room, dressed and ready to go. "Gross! Come on, I'm ready!" Connor cried.

James and I laughed, and I said goodbye to them and brewed some fresh coffee. It was time to finish reading the journal.

* * * * *

My warm mug of coffee sat on the end table next to me as I curled up on the couch. My mother's journal was on my lap, not yet opened. I had already read up until the end of July, which meant a few weeks more of entries until we would have headed home that summer, unless Mom wrote more after that.

Taking a deep breath, I opened to the page after the last entry I had read: August 2nd.

I have been meeting Sam more often this summer and I feel incredibly guilty about it. Johnny seems oblivious and very happy to be playing with his toys, baking with his grandma, or tagging along with his sister and James. Sure, I've made Elise babysit more than she should on her summer break, but my mother is getting older and I don't trust her completely. Not with her hearing fading and the fact that she's slowing down with age and being forgetful.

I asked Sam what would happen next. We leave in a few short weeks. He said it was just a summer fling, but I know better. He feels the same as I do. He just doesn't want to admit it. Maybe he doesn't want children? I'll broach the subject the next time I see him, which is this weekend for dinner in the next town over. I can't wait!

I was sick at what I was reading. So my mom stuck me with Johnny nearly all summer so she could rendezvous with some guy from town? *Sick!* I was so angry I could barely hold onto my coffee mug. I turned the page to the next entry which wasn't dated.

Only two more days until Sam and I go out for dinner! I am so excited. I feel like a teenager again! I'm hoping Mom or Elise will watch Johnny. Sam is picking me up at eight, so Johnny will be tucked into bed by then. I'm meeting Sam at the end of the driveway. I told Mom I was going out with "the girls" from town. Bullshit. If she only knew. Listen to me ... acting like I'm Ellie's age instead of my own adult age! Is this what love is? I don't ever remember feeling like that when

The entry stopped there for some reason. I turned the page, and it was blank. What in the world? A few more blank pages and there was one entry left. It was the date my brother died. *Do I dare read it? Maybe I should wait until later. What if James returns with Johnny and I'm in the middle of it?*

No. I had no choice but to read it. If anything, it's for the sake of closure.

Mom and I had the worst fight the night I was supposed to go to dinner with Sam. She found out, somehow. Probably Gert at the store. Gert should mind her own business. Everyone in this damn town is so nosey! Mom confronted me. I asked what the big deal was because I was a widow and could see whom I chose! She said she knows what I did and ought to be ashamed of myself, especially since Sam was well-respected in the community as well as a good friend of the family. I tried and tried to deny everything, but I couldn't. I blurted it out ... .Sam and I have been seeing each other, and it's been the best time of my life!

I sat there stunned. I couldn't believe what I was reading. Did I really want to continue? Anger was boiling my blood; I could feel it. How could my mother write this stuff so freely? Why didn't she take the journal when she left?? Did she not think because of what happened to Johnny, or did she *want* the journal to be found? *Deep breath and calm down,* I told myself.

Mother was shocked. She asked me if Johnny was Sam's child. I tried to lie. I mean, I did lie. I'm not sure she bought it. Who cares? I'm going out with Sam later this afternoon, and I don't care what anyone thinks. I'm going to tell him once and for all that Johnny is his child. Mom will have to deal. I had an affair, Sam and I were in love, the end! I can only pray she will forgive me, but most of all, Elise. Sweet Elise. She's so sensitive and loved her father dearly. What will she think when she finds out Johnny isn't her father's son?

Even though I had suspected it, reading it from my mother's journal brought every emotion in my body out. I dropped the journal, ran into the bathroom, and threw up. Then I sat on the floor crying. My mother had a terrible secret she kept for years, and she lied to me, my gram, and my father. She even lied to Johnny!!

But what happened the day he died?

Chapter 24

The farmhouse sat before me, surrounded by lovely trees and white fencing, with a few barns in the back of the property. I slowly drove my car up the dirt driveway, and once I parked, I didn't move; I just sat there staring.

The house was beautiful. It was a two-story white structure with multiple windows, a wooden door that seemed like it was made of oak, and a wraparound porch with several chairs and plants. The flowerpots and the ground in front of the house were decked with flowers of many different varieties and colors. I was in awe. It was like looking at a painting—a picture-perfect painting.

I finally slid out of the driver's seat, my feet firmly planted on the ground. *What in the world am I doing here? Where will I start? No—I know what I had to say.* Holding my head up high, I slammed the door shut and began walking towards the gate leading to the house.

"Can I help you?"

Hearing a man's voice, I turned and saw Sam walking towards me from one of the barns. He was dressed in overalls, boots, and a straw hat—ever the farmer.

"Oh, hi, Sam," I said nervously.

"What brings you way out here?"

"I need to talk to you," I answered, putting on my best "firm" voice.

Sam raised his eyebrows. "Ok, sure. Come on, the porch is more comfortable than standing around."

I followed Sam to the porch and sat on one of the comfortable chairs while he planted himself on a rocking chair. I hated rocking chairs.

I sat staring at the trees, their branches slightly swaying in the breeze, until I realized Sam was staring at me. It was now or never.

"Sam, I'm going to be blunt," I started.

"You know, Elise, I'd sure like a cold beer right now. Get you one?" Sam stood up and I nodded. *Fine, if that's what it takes to get him to listen.*

Sam walked back out a few minutes later, holding two bottles of light beer. He handed one to me and sat down with his. I took a swig of mine before continuing.

"My mom had a journal, and I found it at the lake house. I read it all."

Sam didn't say anything, just continued to rock and drink his beer. He had a far-off look on his face. Did he know what I was going to say? Did he have any idea? I plunged ahead anyway.

"I have reason to believe that my brother, Johnny, was—*is*—your son."

Rocking, sipping on beer, more rocking. Why wasn't Sam saying anything? I continued drinking my beer as well. I would wait him out. Minutes passed. An occasional car or truck drove by in the distance, the mooing of cows in the barn could be heard, and—of course—the happy chirping of birds. Why did birds always sound happy?

Finally, Sam spoke. "Let me ask you a question," he said slowly, still not looking at me. "Why now?"

"Why now … what?"

"Why in the world do you want to bring all of this up now?" Sam finally looked at me. His eyes were kind, but I sensed distrust. "Your mother is in an institution, and your brother is dead. So why can't you leave it alone?"

"I—"

"Elise," Sam interrupted. "I am a good citizen, a well-respected man in the community and liked by basically everyone. I've been married for a few years now. My farm has run successfully through the years, despite all this newfangled crap they have with trying to put out good farmers. I don't need any gossip going around about something that happened almost two decades ago."

"So you admit to the affair?"

Sam sighed. He finished his beer and set his bottle down, then stood up and began pacing the porch. "I already did when you first asked me, and I'm sorry about that—the affair. Obviously, I am not a hundred percent innocent in what happened. However, your mother did tell me she and your father had separated."

"What?" I jumped up almost spilling my beer. I set the bottle down and folded my arms across my chest, glaring at Sam. "Why would she say that?"

Sam threw his arms up. "I have no idea! Who knows why people do certain things? I didn't ask; she didn't elaborate. She and I knew each other because she came up hear every year with her parents—your grandparents. We were friends, but at one point it turned into something more. She was already married, so I backed off." Sam stopped pacing and turned to face me. "I never meant to hurt anyone. But I did love her back then. When your father died … well, we picked it back up. Then after you guys left the last summer you were here, I never heard from her again."

"But … wait. So you had the affair, then when you found the truth about my father still being with her, you backed off?"

"Sure did. I told you, Elise, I'm not a bad man."

"Ok, what about Johnny?" I challenged, still not quite believing his side of the story. Of course, it was the *only* side I had actually heard. I had no other proof but what my mother wrote in her journal.

"Yeah, sorry, kid. She never said anything about your brother. If he was mine, I had no idea."

I shook my head and stared off into the distance, watching birds fly from tree to tree. Oh, to be a bird, so free and … .carefree. I didn't know what to do next. Mom had an affair, she never told Sam that Johnny was his son, Johnny is dead, and Mom is incoherent. The end. Right?

I turned back to Sam. "Ok. I guess that's what I wanted to know. I mean, it doesn't answer all of my questions, but there's nothing else to say, is there?"

Sam shook his head. "I'm sorry, hon. If I thought there was a chance Johnny was my kid, I'd want to know and get to know him. Not to sound callused, but I don't see a point since he isn't here."

I nodded. It hurt, but it made sense. Why dredge up everything now for Sam? Pointless.

I thanked Sam and walked back to my car. Honestly, I don't know what I was expecting from him. I couldn't blame him for not being thrilled about having a son or wanting to know about him. Johnny was the result of an affair, whether loveless or not, and Sam had moved on.

I climbed into my car and sat there for a few minutes, staring off into the distance. My mind was trying to process everything, and I wasn't sure if I wanted to scream or cry. I did neither. Instead, I drove away from Sam's house, not looking back, and decided to stop at Gert's for a few groceries before heading to the house. Morgan and Rachel were hanging out, and I didn't expect her home for a few hours. I knew Connor was safe with James.

Gert was busy with customers, but that was ok with me. I wanted to get in and out. That hope was short-lived.

"Elise! How ya doin' today, girl?"

I turned and smiled at Charlie. "Hi, Charlie. I'm ok."

He pulled me into a hug, then pulled back and looked into my eyes. His eyes were kind, his face weathered, and I'm sure I glimpsed a bit of sympathy there.

"Listen, I'm sure you want to talk about … " he began, then quickly turned to make sure we were out of earshot. "You know, your grandma's wishes and all."

"I do," I nodded firmly. "I really want to understand why in the world she'd want to be buried—"

"Yoo hoo! Elise! Come here when you're finished!" Gert called, interrupting us.

I waved in acknowledgement and turned back to Charlie. He gave me a wink and a smile. "Call me." He handed me a card. It was a business card to the stables, and I looked at him gratefully.

"Thank you; I will."

Charlie tipped his hat in old-fashioned cowboy style, then walked away.

Gert hurried to me, handing me a bag. I peeked inside and couldn't help but laugh.

"Gert, what is this?" I asked, holding up the bag full of goodies.

"Oh, hush. I noticed Connor eyeballing these the last time he was in here. Kids love their candy, and I'm sure he hasn't even tried some of these. My treat."

"Thanks, Gert. Talk to you later!" I headed out with a smile, feeling lighter than I had when I left Sam's house.

I had just pulled the car into the driveway, when I saw James pull his truck in behind me. Connor jumped out and ran over.

"Mommy!" Connor enveloped me in a big bear hug. He was sweaty from being in the sun. I hugged him back and looked up at James.

"Did you two have a good time?" I asked, standing up. I pulled a grocery bag out of the car, and James took it from me.

We walked into the house, Connor excitedly telling me about his fishing adventure. "I caught some fish, but I let them go because they were so small," he chattered on. "I caught two big ones, and James said he was going to clean them off and … you know … " Connor made a slicing motion with his finger across his neck, and I laughed.

"Sounds like you had a great day. Why don't you wash up and change clothes? You smell like fish!"

Connor laughed and smelled his hands, then made a face. "Can we go to the beach? I'm hot and want to swim."

"Sure. Go wash up and get changed."

Connor ran off, and I turned to James. "Thanks again for taking him out today."

James reached out to give me a hug, but I laughed and held my hands up. "I'm sure you smell like fish, too," I laughed.

James backed off, laughing. "We had fun. Did you finish the journal?"

"Um … yeah, and then I met with Sam. I went right to his house."

James nodded and leaned against the counter as I put my groceries away. I know he was curious about the conversation between Sam and I, but I wanted to make sure Connor wasn't anywhere in ear shot.

"Let me change quick," I told James. I hurried to my room to put on my suit under shorts and a T-shirt, grabbed the beach bag, and met James in the kitchen just as Connor came bounding downstairs wearing his swim trunks and dragging his towel behind him.

"Ready!" he shouted excitedly.

"Ok, sweetie." I grabbed two beers from the fridge and, after handing one to James, walked out behind Connor. James followed and we made our way to the beach. Connor was raring to go and ran right into the water, laughing when he realized how cold it was. He always did that—ran into the water before testing it. Ahh, to be young and carefree again.

James and I sat on the sand and opened our beers. "Thanks again for taking Connor today," I said to James after taking a sip of the refreshing brew.

"You don't have to thank me. I love spending time with him."

"I knew you'd make a great father. If I had only given you a chance … " I began.

"Ellie—"

"No, no, it's ok. I know. Anyway, I suppose you want to hear about my conversation with Sam."

"Yep." James looked at me expectantly. "Did it go the way you thought?" I shook my head. "Right," he said turning back to the lake.

"I mean, he admitted to the affair and the fact that Johnny could have been his kid, but he didn't want anything to do with the conversation or any of the past."

"Why would he?"

"You're taking his side?"

"No, I'm not taking sides. But why dredge up the past? Your mother isn't even around, and Johnny is—"

"I know, I know. That's what Sam said. I have no idea why I even confronted him. I guess I wanted confirmation that what my mother said is true."

"Now let it go," James whispered, taking my hand. He leaned over and gave me a kiss, and I sighed in contentment.

I think I *was* ready to let it all go. I had to face the facts: there was no changing the past, and I had to make peace with myself.

James and I watched Connor jump in and out of the water like a fish. I was a bit on edge about him swimming without me or his sister since the water was a bit rough, but he was having so much fun.

"Connor said something strange today," James said suddenly.

"What?"

"Well, we were out on the fishing boat and suddenly Connor said something about secrets."

"Ok … "

"He asked me why adults keep secrets. I told him not all adults do, but sometimes adults don't tell kids everything because some things are for adults only."

"That sounds fine. I probably would have said the same thing."

"Only … well … "

"What, James?" I was confused and a little nervous about where the conversation was heading.

"He said, 'Everyone keeps secrets.' I asked him what he meant. He shrugged and said, 'Johnny told me that.'"

Chapter 25

My veins turned to ice, and I nearly dropped my beer bottle. *What the hell?* I looked at James, feeling sick inside. First Connor sees a little boy around—or supposedly sees one—and now he's hearing from my dead brother? He doesn't even know about Johnny!

"James, what is going on?"

"I don't know, Ell. I feel like maybe … well, maybe Connor somehow knows about Johnny, and he's letting his imagination take over. Maybe Morgan said something to him."

"No. No, no, no. This has to stop." I started to stand up.

"Ellie, no." James grabbed my arm and pulled me back next to him. "Don't say anything to Connor. Not now. Let's ask Morgan if she said anything to him."

"Ok." I took a deep breath and tried to calm down. Why wouldn't the nonsense with Connor seeing someone or hearing someone who wasn't really there stop?

"But Ellie," James continued, "at some point you really should tell Connor about your brother. It's not fair to keep that from him. He's a child, but he can handle it. Johnny was his uncle; he has a right to know about him."

I knew James was right; I hated that he was right. I wanted to protect Connor from everything—even knowing about death—but I knew that was silly thinking. I couldn't shelter him forever. Like James said, Johnny was his uncle. I needed to be open with Connor about this and move forward.

* * * * *

"Mom, I swear I never said anything to Connor about Johnny!"

"Ok, ok. Don't get defensive."

"Wouldn't *you?*" Morgan snapped.

I tried to hold my temper. It wasn't Morgan's fault I was angry, and I couldn't take it out on her. Maybe angry was too harsh a word; I was more frustrated than anything.

"Why can't you just tell him you had a brother?" Morgan mumbled. She pushed her toe around in the sand, making figure eights. I took her for a walk to the beach while James played catch with Connor to keep him distracted. I simply asked her if she told her brother anything about Johnny, and she jumped down my throat!

"I never wanted to tell him until he was older. I didn't want him to be afraid of the water like I was."

"You're not afraid of the water," Morgan responded.

"No, not really. I mean, I'll go in the water, but I'm more afraid for you two."

"That's different." Morgan stood up and brushed sand off her shorts. "Are we done? James and I are going to town to get stuff for s'mores tonight."

"Sure, honey."

Morgan was already walking towards the house. James looked over with a quizzical look on his face and I just shrugged. I didn't want to push it. We only had two weeks left at the lake, and I didn't want to ruin her time.

I followed Morgan to the house and sat on the porch swing while she left for town with James. I watched Connor play for a few minutes by the rocks. He looked so happy and innocent. Did I really want to tell him his uncle drowned in this very lake when he was Connor's age? Wouldn't that scare him? No, I had to do it. It was time. No more secrets. I took a deep breath before calling Connor.

"Honey, come here."

"What is it, Mommy?"

Connor ran up the lawn and onto the porch. I patted the seat next to me, and he climbed up on the swing. I pushed the floor with my feet to rock back and forth as I stared out at the lake. The sun was reflecting perfectly off the water. It was a calm day—no breeze or clouds in the sky.

"Connor, I want to tell you something," I began.

"A secret?" he asked, eyes wide.

"No. I mean, well ... sure. But a different kind of secret. A secret Mommy has been keeping from you."

Connor frowned. "That's not nice, Mommy. We aren't supposed to keep secrets."

"I know." I sighed. "But this secret didn't hurt anyone, and I think it's ok to keep some things to ourselves."

"Like grown-up stuff?"

I nodded. "Yeah, sort of like that."

"Ok, Mommy. What is your secret?"

I took a deep breath and looked back to the lake. "Well, when I was a little girl, my mommy had a little boy like you! I was a big sister. His name was—"

"Johnny."

I whipped my head over to look at my son. What did he just say? It was almost a whisper, but I heard it. How did he know my brother's name? "Connor ... what did you say?"

Connor looked up at me. "Nothing, Mommy. I didn't say anything."

I stood up, feeling anxious and a little angry. "Stop fooling around. This isn't funny anymore! I know you just said the name Johnny!"

Connor's eyes widened and he shrugged. "I promise I

didn't say anything!"

I took a deep breath. Clearly, he was not telling the truth, but I had to let it go. *What in the world is going on with him this summer?* I leaned back on the porch rail and finished. "Anyway, his name, as you seem to know, is Johnny."

"So I have an uncle?" Connor asked with a smile.

"No, sweetie. Johnny … well, he died when he was five. He is in Heaven now."

"Oh. How did he die?"

I didn't want to say it, but Connor was big enough to understand. "Honey, he drowned in the lake up here when I was only sixteen, just a teenager like Morgan. Johnny … we … he couldn't swim very well, but the water was rough that day anyway."

"I can swim good!"

"I know you can, sweetie. But this is why I don't ever want you to swim in the lake without someone around … preferably me. Ok? Do you understand now?"

Connor nodded. "I do. So … "

"What, Connor?"

"My uncle must be the person I'm seeing up here. He must be watching over me, but as a little boy because that's when he died!"

My heart skipped a beat, but I didn't say anything. *Was it Johnny's spirit that Connor was seeing this summer?* Could Johnny be watching over my son? My heart warmed at the thought. *Sweet Johnny.* Suddenly, I didn't feel frustrated or angry at what Connor had been saying he saw all summer. Maybe my brother's spirit really was at the lake house, watching over us all.

"Mommy, I'm sorry my uncle died. Can I go play now?"

And that was that. Connor ran back off to his rocks and I flopped back down on the swing. I closed my eyes, thankful the talk was over. It wasn't as bad as I thought it was going to be, and I actually felt a little better. I guess kids are resilient.

"Mom, we got ice cream, too!"

I turned when I heard Morgan's excited voice as she and James returned from town. Connor ran over to them. "Ice cream!" he cried, fist pumping the air.

I laughed and stood to greet her and James. James was carrying two bags full of stuff. I shook my head; I sent them for a few items!

"What in the world?" I asked, laughing.

"Party tonight!" James shrugged with a grin.

"First, swim time!" Morgan cried. She ran inside to change, and Connor ran after her yelling, "Morgan, I had an uncle!"

James looked at me, eyebrows raised. I shrugged and led him inside so we could put the groceries away. "Yeah, I told him. He took it well."

"Good. No more secrets," James said, pulling me into his arms.

Chapter 26

"Hey, Ellie. Do you want to go for a swim?"

"What?"

We were sitting on the porch, drinking our third cup of coffee that morning. James had arrived early so we could take the kids on a hike, and when we returned, Connor crashed on the couch. It was barely ten in the morning; I couldn't blame him. It *was* a nice morning for a hike, though. The air had been just cool enough, so we weren't sweaty and sticky, and the sky was a brilliant blue color. Morgan and Connor enjoyed the hike, but they got up early for it. I was shocked when Morgan agreed to get up early. James was a good influence on her. I'd need him around when school started.

"Let's go to our spot. Remember? Come on, like old times!" His eyes crinkled when he smiled. I loved those eyes.

"James, that beach doesn't exactly bring good memories."

"What? Of course it does! We had a lot of fun times there."

He looked so happy, that I became caught up in his excitement. What would it hurt? Morgan could stay inside while Connor napped. I nodded my "ok" and told James I needed to change, and he left to get his swim trunks.

Good Lord, had I shaved? I quickly checked my legs and sighed with relief. My legs were ok. I ran into my room and pulled out some bathing suits. I chose the light blue tankini, one I hadn't worn in front of the kids. I wasn't sure why; maybe I thought Morgan would think I was trying too hard to be young. But I *was* still young! I pulled the bathing shorts on and then the matching top. Looking in the mirror, I nodded and smiled. Working out and eating well paid off!

I grabbed some towels, sunscreen, and bottled water and threw them in a bag. Before walking out, I found Morgan sitting in a chair in the living room, reading a magazine.

"Honey, James and I are going—"

"Yeah, yeah," Morgan interrupted, looking up from her magazine. "I heard you two. Go have fun. I'll stay here with dork-face." Morgan was grinning, and I said a quick "thanks" and headed out.

James was waiting by the steps wearing nothing but swim trunks. He was still fit after all those years—his chest hard and bronze from the sun. *Oh, man!*

He grinned when he saw me and grabbed the beach bag. "You look amazing!" he said, giving a low whistle.

I rolled my eyes. "You don't look too bad yourself." *Oh my gosh, are we flirting?* "Race you to the beach!" I took off while laughing.

James ran up behind me and playfully slapped my thigh, then ran ahead of me. He always did win when we raced anywhere.

We arrived at our special spot out of breath because, in shape or not, we weren't teenagers anymore. James dropped the bag and walked to the water's edge. It was such a beautiful morning. The sun shone brightly on the lake, refracting it back into my eyes. I had forgotten my sunglasses, but I didn't care.

"We used to come here all the time, remember?" James whispered into my ear. He took my hand and pulled me down onto the sand with him. We sat close and I shivered with delight.

"I remember."

We sat in silence for a while, each lost in our memories. This place—*our place*—was so magical, for so many reasons. Even with that one bad memory from that one fateful summer, our spot was special to me. Back then, it had been the one place I could escape from my mother or little brother—or anything else I wanted to escape from. Sometimes I'd sit here alone, but most of the time it was a place for James and me. We would sit and talk for hours, swim, kiss …

All of a sudden, I felt cold water come over my body. I looked up in shock and saw James grinning. He had splashed me!

"*Ohh,* this means war," I threatened with a grin.

I jumped up and kicked water at him, then ran away laughing. He followed me into the water, practically tackling me. We laughed and splashed, then swam, acting like the teenagers we once were—carefree, worry-free. I let all negative emotions seep out of me as I grinned and laughed like a teenager.

After spending some time splashing and swimming in the water, we sat on our towels and guzzled bottled water. The sun was high in the sky at that point, and the temperature must have been at least 90 degrees.

"I bet you haven't laughed like that in a while," James commented after finishing his water.

I smiled at him. He was right. I hadn't laughed like that since … well, probably since I was here with him all those years ago. Sure, Greg and I had some good times, and I used to laugh when the kids were younger, but it wasn't the carefree laugh I was enjoying then with James.

"You're right. I haven't."

"Were you happy, Ell? I mean, with Greg?"

I nodded slowly. What could I say? "It was … different." James waited, so I continued. "I met him through my aunt's friend. He was her friend's nephew, actually. He was older than I was—mid-twenties to my eighteen years—but he was successful and grounded, and he was kind. He treated me well, and I did love him … I just didn't *fall* in love with him. Does that make sense?" I looked at James, anxious for his response.

"It does. I'm glad you had someone who loved you and Morgan and took care of you, though I won't lie—it does make me feel a little jealous." I swat his arm playfully. "Seriously, though. I get it. I dated a couple women, but I could never get serious. I probably sound like a loser, but I was always waiting for someone who could make me feel the way you used to make me feel. I know we were young, just teens, but I loved you, Ell."

"I know. And I loved you … always have. But I was so scared to look for you after therapy and getting on my feet—finishing high school with an infant—and not sure if you even wanted me after not hearing from you."

"That was so wrong; my calls and letter never reaching you." James shook his head and sighed.

"Well, it turned out ok, didn't it? I mean, I was sad that Greg died—it was unexpected—but good things can come from bad, right?"

"They sure can." James smiled and then leaned in close. I knew he was going to kiss me, and I wanted it. I had missed his kisses from so long ago, and his touch! He kissed me slowly and gently, and we both let go of the past, the lies, and the secrets. We held onto each other while letting go of everything else. When we pulled apart, James had that goofy boyish grin on his face, and I couldn't help but laugh.

"We're going to do this right this time," he told me, becoming serious.

"What?"

"This—*us*. We're going to do things the right way. I

want to be married to you before we—well, you know … commit to anything further."

"James—you mean … I—"

James pulled me close and kissed me gently. "I'm not going anywhere. This time, us … forever. I am the father of your daughter and I want to be a father to Connor. You, me, the kids … a family. I'm not letting you get away this time."

I began to cry then, but they were tears of joy. I couldn't believe my life was coming together so beautifully after all I had been through. I loved this man more than anything. "I love you," I whispered.

We sat and held each other, looking out at the lake. The water was gently lapping against the shore, and the bright sun made the water sparkle as though in celebration of our presence.

James broke the spell by standing up and pulling me to my feet. "We better get back," he told me. "Connor is probably awake and itching to go swimming."

I laughed because I knew it would be true. We packed up our belongings and headed up to the house.

Chapter 27

We only had a week before heading home, and there was one final thing I had to take care of. I left Connor with James one day, while Morgan was working, and headed to town to meet with Tom, the attorney who saw to Grandma's will. I was a nervous wreck. *Do I really want to know what is in that will? Yes. I need closure.*

The office was small, in a corner building at the edge of town, but very inviting. Dark wood floors and soft colors on the walls with a few paintings gave a calming effect that people would need when consulting with an attorney.

I walked up to the reception desk where a pretty, young woman sat. She smiled up at me, and I introduced myself, nervously smoothing my shirt, though there were no wrinkles.

"Sure, he'll be with you in a moment."

I sat down, trying to keep my legs from bouncing up and down. There were magazines on a glass coffee table, but I couldn't pick one up. I wanted to stay focused.

"Elise?"

I jumped up when I heard a man's voice say my name. Standing in the doorway of the waiting room was a tall, dark-haired man, with dark eyes and a kind smile. I immediately felt at ease.

"Hi, yes, I'm Elise." I shook Tom's hand and followed him into his office.

I declined coffee and got right down to the matter. "I want to know exactly what my grandma stated in her will regarding—well, where she wanted to be buried. Surely that cannot be legal!"

Tom nodded slowly. "I knew you'd come back someday. Your grandmother knew you would. You know she left you the house."

I nodded. That's the reason I was up at the lake house. My aunt had told me Grandma was in a nursing home, pretty much dying, and I had never heard from her—never received her letters—so I had thought she was angry at me for running off that day when Johnny drowned. I always thought it was my fault. When I received a letter from a lawyer's office—Tom's, actually—it stated my grandmother had passed and her wish was for me to come up to the lake house for one summer and then I could keep it or sell it.

"Well, your grandmother visited me one day to secure her will and she was adamant about being buried there and not in a cemetery. She said she had unfinished business there—whatever that means—and needed to be close to family."

"But … is it legal? I mean, of course it is, if you allowed it. Right?" I was so confused.

"It's legal," Tom assured me. He sat back in his leather chair, rolling a pen between his hands. "There are zoning laws, of course, yadda, yadda, but this is a small town, and we all know each other. We didn't think twice about her request."

I nodded but didn't say anything. I didn't feel right about her body being buried on our land, but if that's what she wanted …

"I knew your family, Elise. I know this is hard for you to digest, but your grandmother was of a perfectly sound mind when she made this request. I only wish she had told someone she was still living there. People could have helped."

"I will never understand it," I said. "I think she thought it was her punishment. Never leave."

"Because of the drowning," Tom put in.

"Because of the drowning," I confirmed.

"Well, is there anything else? You have the paperwork for her accounts and the house."

"Nothing else. Thank you for your time."

"My pleasure."

We stood and shook hands again. I turned to leave when a thought hit me.

"Tom?"

"Yes?"

"Was she buried in something, like a casket?"

"Sort of. It was a casket of sorts. A simple box, really. She didn't want anything extravagant. Right near the rock edge towards the end where the two biggest rocks sit."

"Ok … " That was all I wanted to know. I left Tom's office feeling sad, but at least I had more information.

As I drove home, I really felt I could let the past go. Grandma had her wish met, to be buried on the land, and I was coming to peace with everything. It was time to move forward and only look back at happy memories—not secrets or lies. I still wanted to move her body—er, casket—so new owners wouldn't have to have her there (creepy!). Maybe I'd have her buried next to Johnny.

Chapter 28

As summer was ending, it felt bittersweet. I had discovered ugly things this summer, but I had reunited with James. I also felt I made peace with the past. Well, as much peace as I could. I would always hurt for Johnny and my grandma, but I had to let them rest.

I hadn't forgotten my mother in the institution, I just couldn't visit her. She didn't recognize me at all; she didn't talk when I was there. I knew I should at least try—go and talk to her—but I found I couldn't. After this summer and learning about the past … well, I definitely wouldn't be visiting her. Not until I forgave her for what she had done to our family. That would take some time. I would probably end up seeing a counselor once we got home, just to talk it through and get help with the forgiveness issue.

On Saturday, I decided to take the kids into town to get lunch and do a little shopping. Connor would want to pick out a few last-minute souvenirs.

We ate lunch at a restaurant along the water, then walked through town, poking around the shops. I let them pick out a souvenir for their best friends at home, and they bought a few things for themselves. Connor was obsessed with anything to do with fish, thanks to James taking him fishing over the summer. I'd definitely have to buy him a fishing pole when we got home so he could fish—hopefully with James. I wasn't into worm bait, fish guts, or anything like that.

We were walking in and out of shops, talking and laughing easily, when suddenly, Gert's shop door flew open, and she started running towards us.

"Ellie! Wait!" she cried, out of breath.

"Gert, is everything ok?"

Gert stood for a minute catching her breath. "Yes. I mean, I'm fine, but ... well, you know Sam Davis, right?"

"Oh, um ... yes," I replied cautiously.

Gert nodded. "I thought so. Some locals spotted you two having lunch one day."

Of course they did.

"Anyway, Ellie ... Sam's farm hand found him dead as a doornail on his front porch recently!"

"Oh my goodness! That's terrible!" I hadn't been crazy about Sam, but I wouldn't have wished him dead. And to drop dead just like that? He wasn't that old; what could have happened?

"Yes, ma'am. His wife wanted an autopsy, naturally, and turns out he had a heart attack."

"Well, that's normal, right?" Connor was becoming fidgety, and Morgan was staring at her phone. I'd have to try to wrap the conversation up.

"You'd think so," Gert continued. "They actually looked through medical records, and it turns out he had a heart condition! Apparently, it's genetic. His father had it and was a twin, actually, but the twin died when he was just five years old."

What?? A heart condition ... genetic? My own heart began to race. Could Johnny have had the same condition? Could that have been the cause of his drowning that day?

"Elise, dear, are you ok? You're awfully pale," Gert said, taking my hand in concern.

"*Mommy* ... " Connor whined, itching to continue our

shopping.

I took a deep breath and tried to focus. "I'm ok, sorry. It's just … it's a shock, that's all. His poor wife," I mumbled.

"Well, anyway, calling hours are tomorrow at ten if you can make it. I have to run, Ell," Gert said, letting go of my hand. "Goodbye, kids!" Gert waved and walked back to the store.

We continued our shopping, but my mind stayed on Sam the entire time.

* * * * *

The next day, James came over a little after nine in the morning to attend Sam's calling hours with me. I had called James Saturday when the kids and I returned from town, and we talked a little about what happened to Sam. I realized that even if my little brother had that genetic heart condition from Sam's family, it didn't matter anymore since he wasn't alive, but my heart hurt not knowing, too.

"You look beautiful." James found me in the living room pulling on my black sandals. I hoped they'd be ok for the funeral home. I hadn't brought much for dressing up this summer. How would I know I'd have to attend calling hours for someone?

"You look pretty nice yourself," I smiled as James gave me a kiss on the cheek. He was wearing dark jeans with a long-sleeve button-down shirt of the most stunning deep blue color I had ever seen. I would have rather stayed at the lake house, drinking coffee with James and snuggling instead of going to calling hours.

We walked into the kitchen to have a cup of coffee before heading out. Morgan, at one point, shuffled in, still sleepy-eyed.

"What on earth will you do when school starts up again?" I laughed, and James gave her a hug. Morgan never was a morning person.

She poured coffee into her favorite sunflower mug,

adding caramel-flavored creamer, then flopped in the chair at the table, rubbing her eyes. "How long will you be?" she asked. "Today is going to be a perfect beach day, I think."

"You're right. It's going to be in the low 90's," James told her.

"Not long, honey. No more than an hour, I would say. Thank you for staying here with Connor. I didn't want to take him. He'd be bored," I said. *And probably traumatized if it was open casket,* I thought. "Promise me no swimming until we get back," I added sternly.

"I know, I know," she mumbled.

"Come on, Ell. We better get going," James said, setting his empty mug in the sink.

"Ok. I'll just grab my purse." I gave Morgan a quick kiss on her forehead before leaving the room. I was nervous about leaving the kids, but Morgan was plenty old enough to babysit, and we wouldn't be gone that long. Nothing could happen in that short hour.

I followed James to his truck, and he opened the door for me. I climbed in and took in the scent of his cologne. *Ahh, I love that smell.*

"Ready?" he asked as he started the truck.

"As I'll ever be."

* * * * *

Calling hours was uneventful, thankfully (what had I been expecting?), and James and I only stayed as long as we thought proper, talking to some of the locals and paying respects to Sam's wife and other family members who showed up. It had been a great turnout; Sam had been well-known and respected in the community. His wife was … well, she was a little standoffish, and I wondered if Sam had told her about me or my mom. I doubted it.

"You ok?"

I looked over at James and smiled. We were heading back to the lake house, and I was happy the event was over.

"I'm good. Really." I looked out the open window, the

wind tossing my hair about. "I'm going to let the dead rest once we leave here. Sam, my grandma, Johnny … "

"Good. You need peace," James agreed.

"I can't believe I held onto heartache all these years," I admitted.

"Well, rightfully so. You'll never get over a loved one's death; not completely. However, you can let good memories remain in your heart and leave the bad behind."

"I know." I sighed, absentmindedly rubbing my face.

I stared off into the distance as we passed beautiful trees, the lake just beyond. The sky was darkening with clouds, and I hoped it would clear so the kids could spend more time at the beach.

"I also need to stop playing the 'who is to blame game' because it doesn't matter. I can't hold onto guilt anymore," I added.

"Wise woman," James cracked.

I playfully nudged him and closed my eyes until we reached the lake house.

We finally pulled into the driveway, and James let me out. He wanted to go home and change before meeting us at the beach. "I'll walk back over through the woods," he told me.

"Ok, thanks. See you in a bit!" I waved to James and hurried inside, anxious to see my kids.

Chapter 29

No one was inside, but I did notice Morgan's scented candles burning on one of the tables near the back door. I couldn't count the number of times I told Morgan to blow out candles when she was not going to stay in the room!

I opened the back door and was relieved to see Connor and Morgan hanging out on the back porch playing cards.

"Mommy!" Connor jumped up and ran over to give me a hug. "Beach time now, right?"

I grinned. He was still in his sleep clothes, and it was almost noon. "You need to change first, and I need to change and pack a beach bag. James is coming with us, and I want to spend the entire day there. Well, as much time as we can. It's getting cloudy, so I'm not sure if it will rain."

"I'm ready," Morgan said. She had her suit on under her shorts and shirt. "Just going to grab my beach bag and head down."

As she walked into the house, I shouted after her. "Blow out those candles, please!" I reached for Connor's hand. "Ok, buddy, let's go get ready."

Connor and I went inside as Morgan was heading back out. She probably wanted to work on her tan before her "pesky" little brother joined her. I totally got that.

Connor ran to his room to change as I hurried to my bedroom. After changing, I went to the kitchen to make sandwiches. I wanted to pack chips and apples as well. The beach was close to the house, but who wanted to run back for snacks?

A glance out the window told me there were still clouds in the sky. Darn it. Maybe the clouds would pass, and the sun would be completely out for the rest of the day. The forecast hadn't called for rain.

"Mommy, I'm ready!" Connor appeared behind me wearing his swim trunks and was holding sunscreen in one hand and goggles in another.

"Ok, but you have to wait for me." I threw two bags of chips in a bag along with four apples. I still needed to put the sandwiches and drinks in the cooler.

"But Morgan is there," he whined.

"Can't you wait a few minutes?"

"Please? I'll be careful!"

I sighed. *I guess it won't hurt.* "Ok, honey, but please don't go into the water just yet. Wait for me, ok? The water seems rough today. See those clouds?"

"I know, Mommy. I won't go in, I promise!"

"Ok," I agreed, against my better judgement. "No water!"

Connor huffed but mumbled an "ok" while running out the back door. It took me a short while to fill the cooler with ice and put the sandwiches and drinks inside. I then filled a bag with towels and Connor's pail and shovel so he could build a sandcastle.

After I used the bathroom and filled my arms with everything, I began to head towards the back door. I was regretting letting the kids go ahead of me since I was stuck carrying everything out by myself.

All of a sudden, I heard a blood-curdling scream.

I stood still, rooted in place. My heart was beating wildly, but I could not move.

It was after I heard my daughter scream, "Connor!"

that I bolted to the rear door. While running, I tossed the items I was holding and heard a crash, but I couldn't think about that; I had to see what was happening!

I threw the back door open and ran towards the beach. The sky seemed darker, and I noticed the lake water was rough from the wind.

I spotted Morgan in the water, and Connor ... *where is Connor? WHERE IS MY SON?*

I began screaming Connor's name as Morgan swam. What was she swimming towards? Was Connor in the water? The wind had picked up and the water was so rough!

I looked up as I ran and saw James sprinting out of the woods toward the beach. Tears were running down my face, and I was shouting for my kids. *Where is Connor?*

As I neared the beach, I noticed that James—who was still running a little ahead of me—glanced behind me. His face contorted in horror, but he kept running to the water.

I spun around to see what he was looking at, and the last thing I saw before everything went black were flames shooting out of the lake house.

Epilogue

Light rain began to fall from the sky, but I stood before the gravestones, my eyes closed, and my face lifted to Heaven.

Peace washed over me, and I felt comforted that my loved ones were together. I had cried for days, but it was time to let go. It was hard when you didn't get closure—when someone you love dies so suddenly you feel as if your heart was torn from your body. But … I knew I'd be ok.

I knelt before the graves and laid flowers in front of each stone. I wouldn't hold on to this like I did the other deaths in my life. No, this one I would let go.

I took a deep breath and blew one last kiss to the graves, tears streaming down my cheeks. My heart didn't ache so much anymore.

Suddenly, a small hand touched my shoulder. I smiled and turned around.

With a smile on his face, my son asked, "Mommy, are you ready to go home?"

"I am, sweetie. I am." I stood up, and Connor put his small hand in mine as we walked towards the car where James
and Morgan were waiting.

As we drove away, I glanced back at the cemetery, silently saying "goodbye" to my grandma, mother, and Johnny.

I was told my mother had died peacefully in her sleep. I was asked if I wanted an autopsy done on her, but I declined. My mother didn't need anything done to her; she was at rest, and that's all I had wanted for her.

As for Grandma, well … I couldn't leave her at the lake house—or what was left of it. I didn't want her alone there. She needed to be with family. I know your body stays behind and your soul goes to Heaven (I had also made peace with God after He spared my son's life at the lake), but I wanted "her" to be with my mother and Johnny.

I was thinking how grateful I was to have my little family. I was lucky, indeed. I could have lost my son that day at the lake house, but God had other plans.

Morgan told me that Connor did, in fact, go into the water alone because he dropped his floaty and wanted to grab it before the water took it away. He couldn't swim well without his floaties, so the rough water grabbed him, pulling him out. Morgan swam fast to reach him but the rough water proved to be almost too much. Suddenly, Connor's body was thrust towards her, and she was able to grab his arm. Connor insists that he felt small hands pushing him towards his sister, and I believe him. He told me "Uncle Johnny" rescued him.

I honestly believe my little brother's spirit was sent as Connor's guardian angel that summer and assisted in saving my son's life. I also believe my grandmother's spirit had been with us during the summer as well, pushing me to find my mother's journal and forcing me to go back to the past so I could finally put everything to rest.

As for the lake house ... well, it burned to the ground that day. Apparently, as I was running outside, I knocked over the stand that held Morgan's candles. And you know what? I don't regret that at all. My mother was right: the place needed to be burned to the ground. Good riddance.

The kids and I went home after that awful day at the lake house, and James stayed at his cabin until it was cleaned and locked up until he could sell it. We never wanted to return to that town anyway. Of course, I'd keep in touch with Gert through phone calls and letters, but as for the town itself, I was done.

A month after we came home, James and I were married in a small chapel, and we were now living as a happy family. James and I even talked about having a baby one day soon. Morgan was skeptical, but Connor was over the moon at the thought of having a younger sibling to "boss around."

My lies and secrets had been unveiled that summer—as

were my mother's and even my grandmother's—but our story had a happy ending after all.

About the Author

In addition to being an author, Melanie Lopata is an editor and the owner/operator of Get It Write Publishing.

www.GetItWritePublishing.Company

In addition to writing books and running a publishing company, Melanie has a blog called As Real As It Gets and a YouTube channel where she vlogs. She also loves to read and spend time with family.

Follow Melanie on social media.

www.Instagram.com/Melanielynnlopata

www.facebook.com/MelaniesBooks

www.facebook.com/GetItWritePublishingCompany

www.MelanieLynnCollection.com

YouTube: @AsRealAsItGetsML